Sick! Sick! Sick!
Robert Essig

Infected Voices Publishing

Copyright © 2023 by Robert Essig

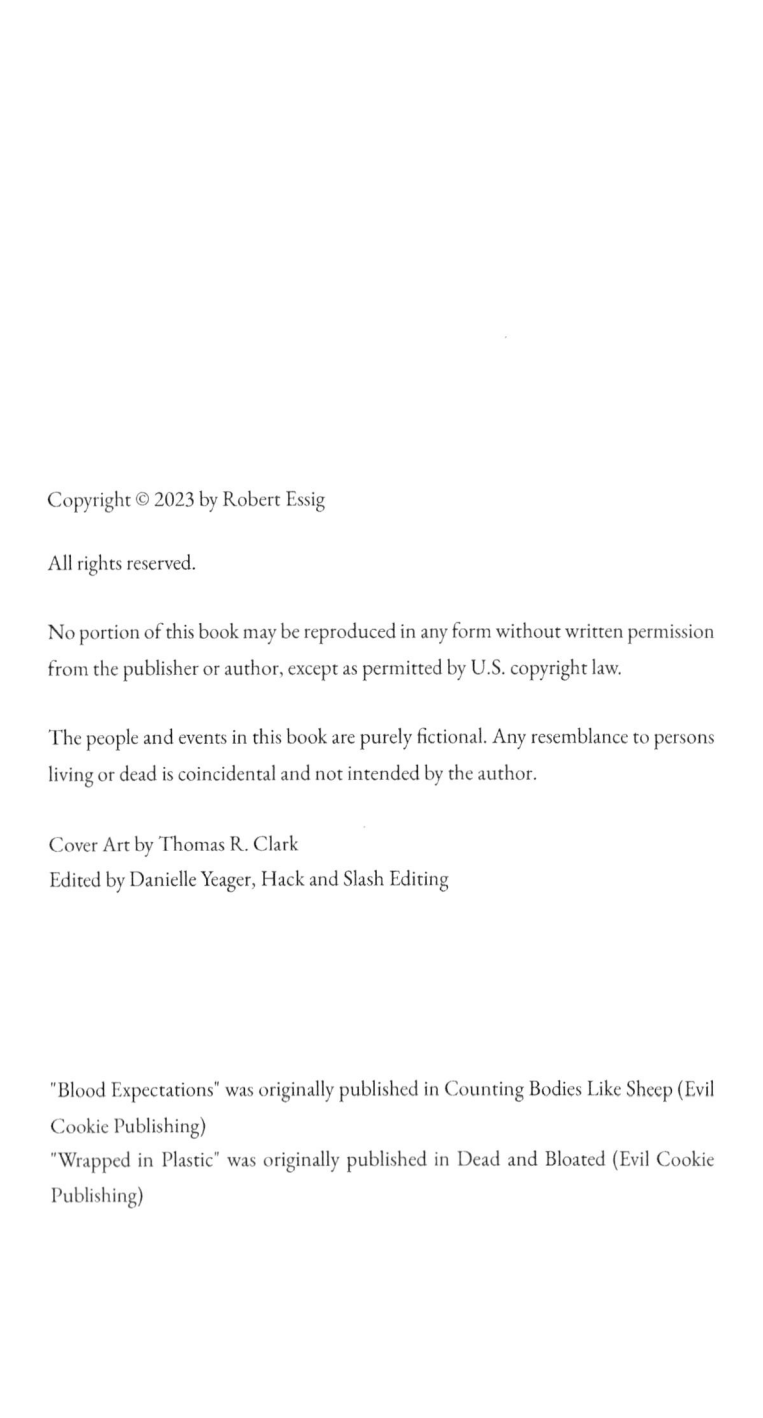

All rights reserved.

No portion of this book may be reproduced in any form without written permission from the publisher or author, except as permitted by U.S. copyright law.

The people and events in this book are purely fictional. Any resemblance to persons living or dead is coincidental and not intended by the author.

Cover Art by Thomas R. Clark
Edited by Danielle Yeager, Hack and Slash Editing

"Blood Expectations" was originally published in Counting Bodies Like Sheep (Evil Cookie Publishing)
"Wrapped in Plastic" was originally published in Dead and Bloated (Evil Cookie Publishing)

Contents

1. 120 Days — 1
2. Vengeance of The Donut Man — 20
3. My 6000 Pound Wife — 32
4. Blood Expectations — 45
5. Blowout — 57
6. Pacify Her — 71
7. Wrapped in Plastic — 82

120 Days

Part One

Samantha insisted he go downtown to Rochester's Jewelry to get her ring refitted since that was where he bought the ring for her ten years ago. Kyle argued that it didn't matter where he went, but Samantha was adamant, claiming that since they made the ring in the first place, they'd be the best for a good refitting without fucking up the stability of the band or some shit like that.

A ring's a ring, Kyle thought as he blazed down the highway. He knew the exit was coming up but couldn't remember exactly which one it was. He'd brought her ring in the other day. Deciding that it really didn't matter which jeweler he took it to, he pulled off and found one about halfway from their house to fancy pants Rochester's downtown.

Kyle had been such a tool when he bought Samantha her engagement ring. He found one of the most expensive places he could and put the wedding rings on credit that took him as long to pay off as a goddamned car. Hell, her rings cost more than the car he'd been driving at the time! It wasn't like he would have gotten her a Cracker Jack ring or something, but come on. Eight grand?

He shook his head as he pulled off the freeway. He'd thought buying such an expensive ring would be a gesture of his love. He knew how women were. It was all about how many carats and the cost over what the ring actually symbolized.

It symbolized their love.

Or at least it had back when Kyle bought the thing and proposed marriage. As of late, they'd been in a massive slump. So much had changed between them in the ten years since they tied the knot. Distances grew larger. She sometimes spent more time with her work friends. He spent more time playing stupid video games. They'd become irritable with one another to the point they could hardly talk about anything without contention.

The very reason Kyle had taken the ring for refitting in the first place was because he said, "Well, maybe if you lost some weight, the damn thing wouldn't have needed to be cut off your fucking finger."

He'd regretted the comment as soon as it fled his mouth like a runny squirt of verbal diarrhea. Whereas Samantha usually had something quick to come back at him with, she merely cried. His attempts at soothing her had been shrugged off. Kyle wanted to chalk it up to his wife being a bitch, but he'd gone too far. Her weight was something he knew she struggled with, something she was very much ashamed of. He normally danced around the subject, but they'd been in a good rager of an argument and it just sort of came out. They knew each other's soft spots.

By the time Kyle got out of Hamil Brothers Jewelers, he was mentally exhausted. The Hamil brother behind the counter billed him almost twice the quoted price for the refitting, claiming they had trouble blending the metal to the existing band, yadda yadda yadda. Kyle didn't want to hear any of it. He'd been quoted a price, and that's what he expected to pay. Sure, maybe it would be a little more, but *twice* what they quoted ... Fuck that.

He stepped outside with the bag in his hand containing a cheap jewelry box and Samantha's ring, resized to fit her plumper digits. The remark Kyle had made about losing weight so her ring didn't need to be cut off rang through his mind. He'd said plenty of things he regretted, but that one took the cake. It was such a low blow. Despite all the shit they'd been through, Samantha didn't deserve that. Beyond their marital problems, she was a good woman and he knew it.

Standing outside collecting his thoughts after what seemed like an hour of arguing with a hard-nosed jeweler about proper business etiquette, Kyle noticed the business next door. The sign said "The Retro Dungeon" and then in smaller text, "VHS, DVDs, Retro Games, Vintage Books."

Inside, the place was decorated with old posters for Nintendo games and movies like *Big Trouble in Little China* and *Beastmaster*. The guy behind the counter glanced at Kyle and grunted out a noncommittal greeting of some sort. Along the walls were sections of cassette tapes, records, NES games, VHS movies, and vintage T-shirts. Everything Kyle thought a retro pop culture store would sell. A lot of cool stuff, but way overpriced as far as he was concerned. He wasn't into collecting vintage stuff anyway. He just figured he'd take a stroll down memory lane.

The center aisles were filled with more of the same, towering clear to the ceiling, which gave off an almost claustrophobic effect. Kyle wandered through the labyrinthine shelves of Sega Genesis games and laser discs until he found himself at the back of the store, where up against a cinder block wall painted white was a red velvet curtain resembling the common entrance to the adult section back in the days of mom and pop video stores. Instead of an "Adults Only" sign, this curtain had a different sign that said "120 Days."

Kyle tilted his head as he examined the strange accoutrement, so out of place in a store so helplessly dedicated to nostalgia. This back wall was free of vintage posters and product. Kyle turned and realized that, somehow, he couldn't even see the front of the store. Behind him were rows upon rows of old big box porno movies. On closer inspection, they were worse than what he remembered from when he was a kid and snuck into

SICK! SICK! SICK!

the adult section. One box showed a woman deep-throating what appeared to be a donkey. Another was called *On the Rag* and had a picture of a naked girl all bloody between her legs. A second nude girl stood beside her with a blood-bloated tampon in her mouth, the white string dangling from her crimson lips. And yet another video called *Butt Stuff* had a grainy photo of a woman with her face crammed into the cleft of a man's ass, feces smeared over her nose and cheeks like a baby in a high chair eating chocolate cake.

Kyle wasn't entirely certain how he'd wandered into this part of the store. He couldn't help but wonder if children could just as easily wander back here. He and Samantha hadn't had any children, and he figured that ship had sailed, but anything could happen. It wasn't like they were using protection. Of course, their sex life wasn't anything to boast about either. It wasn't so much the weight she'd gained, but that they were drifting apart. Sometimes he felt like he didn't even know his wife anymore.

The red velvety curtain tempted Kyle. Considering he was in the vintage porn section, and these movies were more risqué than your average skin flick, whatever was behind the curtain had to be ten times worse. And what did "120 Days" mean?

There was only one way to find out. Kyle used his hand to open the curtain and peek inside. Through a slender open doorway was a small hall with a couple of trouble lights strung overhead, casting eerie illumination. Kyle looked over his shoulder once more, confirming nobody was there, and then he slipped into the creepy corridor. It was like finding the restroom in some sleazy punk club, minus the annoying amount of band stickers coating the walls like vinyl wallpaper. The next door was akin to that of a walk-in freezer, minus the industrial strength handle. In fact, there was no handle to speak of. Just a slab of steel that looked as cold as it was to the touch. Kyle pushed. It opened on greased hinges, the seal breaking to allow some kind of strange music to escape. Kyle paused as if he was doing something wrong, then continued to open the door and peer inside.

Warmth radiated from the opening. And the unmistakable smell of sex hung heavy in the air like the place was perfumed with it. Something in that smell caused Kyle's loins to stir. And then he opened the door a bit wider, threatening to step inside, when he realized that the music was low and pushed to the background. What he'd been hearing as the seal to the steel door opened was a chorus of moaning pleasure, a din of delight. So many voices moaning and squealing as if some kind of king-sized orgy was taking place.

And that's basically what was happening.

Kyle stepped forward. He felt all kinds of wrong in doing so. He was overdressed for the occasion, for one, but what he saw once he was inside was very different than any orgy he'd have expected, for these people were all dressed in various leather garments. Whips and chains and floggers abound. Melted candle wax over tits and dicks and balls and assholes stretched open like wet mouths. Abrasions, bruises, choking, cock rings. One woman was wrapped in cellophane, her breasts dangling free, nipples jutting and glistening. It was a wonder she could breathe with that huge cock being crammed down her throat.

"Oh, you're new," a voice said, pulling Kyle's attention away from the psychosexual display surrounding him. "Follow me."

The man who'd spoken was wearing nothing but assless chaps. He was sculpted out of granite the color of caramel and glossy like a bodybuilder coated with baby oil that really accentuated his muscles. He began walking, and for reasons he didn't quite understand, Kyle followed.

As they walked, he snuck glances at the bizarre sexual acts being performed all around him. Slapping. Paddles. Moaning. As they rounded a corner, he saw several men gathered around something on a table. They were all thrusting into the object, but there was no way it could be a woman. They were taking it on all sides, and there was blood.

Blood!

Then a man made the most obnoxious sound, which caused Kyle to turn his head as he was still following the bronze guy with the clipboard and assless chaps. The fellow who moaned shot his load in a woman's face and then proceeded to slap her cheeks with his dick.

"This is the changing room," Assless Chaps said. "There are no assigned lockers. When you come here, you choose one, just like at a gym or whatever. If you brought your own gear, that's great. If not, over on that wall we have quite an assortment; everything you could ask for. Then you're all set. Just remember one thing. Here at the 120 Days Club, there are no safe words."

The man offered a smile that was somewhere between vile and devious. Kyle nodded, suddenly feeling like he was in over his head. How the hell had he ended up in this place?

Assless Chaps walked away, glancing over his shoulder at Kyle as he rounded the corner and ventured back into the maelstrom of bodies. Kyle wasn't sure about the way that man looked at him. The look wasn't so much carnal as it was predatory.

There were benches, just like in a sports locker room. Kyle set the bag with Samantha's ring on the closest one. He examined the lockers, noticing that some of them had rings hanging from those little hooks one might hang a towel from. He looked closely, realizing they were wedding rings.

What the fuck?

Crossing the room, he made his way to the wall of implements. Fucking hell! Leather gimp suits, harnesses, masks, corsets, and chokers hung on display like the implements of pain rather than pleasure. One section was adorned with an assortment of whips, chains, floggers, and bridles. Another bin was filled with dildos and vibrators in a veritable rainbow of colorful options and flesh-gaping sizes. And everything was slick and greasy, which just about made Kyle vomit.

The hollow leather suits reminded him of executioners, as did the masks. And the whips and floggers didn't resemble anything that he would have associated with pleasure. They were implements of torture, as confirmed by the cries he was beginning to hear slip through the moans of pleasure. He looked at his phone to see what time it was. How long had he been out? Samantha would be expecting him home. It had been perhaps an hour longer than he should have spent, which wasn't a big deal, but he needed to leave. This place made him feel an intense draw to his vanilla home life.

"Here at the 120 Days Club, there are no safe words."

Kyle and Samantha didn't have a safe word. They didn't need one. Their love wasn't one that teetered on violence. Kyle couldn't understand how people got off on this kind of shit.

What the fuck are you doing? What if someone takes a picture of you? What then? What will Samantha think?

As Kyle stood there, the sounds intensified. What he at first thought of as moans of carnal ecstasy were rapidly turning to cries of agony. Frightened whimpers. Fear.

He took off in the direction he and Assless Chaps had come from. This time, he didn't look at anyone as he rushed through the throng of fucking and sucking and torture. He heard it all. The slurping and the muffled cries. He felt all their eyes upon him as he beelined for the exit. As he passed the men huddled around something bloody, he could swear it was a woman with holes cut into her body. He only saw the scene from the corner of his eye, but their thrusting cocks were slathered in blood and chunks of gore.

No. It can't be. I'm just fucking losing it.

He made it to the door, fearing there would be some kind of bouncer there who would give him that same mischievous look ol' Assless Chaps had given him—the look that would incite pain over pleasure. But no one was there.

Kyle opened it into the little cinder block hallway and fled through the velvet curtain. He just about knocked over a collection of vintage horror films in clamshell cases as he navigated his way through the floor-to-ceiling shelves and out of the store.

It wasn't until he stepped foot in the house that he realized he'd left the bag with Samantha's wedding ring on the bench in that vile locker room.

Part Two

The following day, Kyle found himself back at The Retro Dungeon. He'd convinced Samantha that the ring hadn't been ready yet. After a sleepless night trying to figure out how to rectify the situation, Kyle determined he would have to make a return visit to the bizarre sex club and hope the people who frequented the place weren't thieves. Or maybe there was a lost and found. Kyle imagined a bin with greasy butt plugs and dildos he'd have to rummage through to find the goddamned jewelry box.

The same guy sat behind the counter inside, leafing through some old comic book. He looked just as bored as yesterday. Kyle wondered how much he knew about the 120 Days Club. He wondered if the man was judging him.

Though he knew exactly where he was going, Kyle pretended to browse as if he wasn't headed straight for the S&M club hidden in the back of the place. Did the others do the same, or was there no shame in their game? Was the club even open? And why the fuck was there a sex club hidden away in a fucking retro games and comics store?

Pushing his way through the velvet curtain, Kyle entered the slender hallway. The door stood like a slab of steel someone might perform an autopsy on. He pushed. It opened. Kyle walked in. Today, the place was quiet. There was no one in sight. No music. No moans of passion or cries of pain. Nothing.

Making his way toward the locker room, Kyle's eyes lingered on his surroundings. Sex swings dangled like leather hammocks. Stained mattresses were staggered like castoffs from an eviction. His eyes lingered on the stains. Cum and smears of mascara. And blood. Unmistakably blood, dark like chocolate syrup, but this wasn't the type of place that hosted banana split parties.

As he closed in on the locker room area, he saw the mattress that had been on his mind all night, the one where he'd swore he saw men fucking holes cut into a woman's body. It was but a glimpse, for he didn't want to be caught staring, but he knew what he'd seen. They were cramming their erections into gashes cut in her flesh. He couldn't tell whether she was alive or not. How could she have been alive? Who would give consent to have holes cut in their body and allow men to fuck said holes? She would have been in need of serious medical attention.

The mattress they had used was like the one in *Hellbound: Hellraiser II* that the mentally deranged man sits upon when he opens the puzzle box, only worse. It was wet. So saturated with blood that it hadn't dried from the day before. As Kyle passed, he could smell it, and he began to question his judgment in coming back to this place.

In the locker room, leather suits hung like shed skins along one wall in an unsettling display. Floggers, whips, chains, and other instruments of pleasure through pain hung on hooks. The quiet of the place unnerved Kyle. He wanted to get out of there. All he needed was Samantha's ring.

But the little bag from the jeweler wasn't atop the bench that flanked the series of lockers hanging askew just like he remembered from high school gym class.

Fuck!

The absolute stillness of the place was disturbed by a sound coming from somewhere farther in the facility than he'd gone yesterday. It was a squishing noise punctuated by low moans and what sounded kind of like air escaping.

Kyle made his way deeper into the locker room, scanning every surface for the little bag he'd brought in yesterday, hoping that someone who had stumbled upon it had moved it so they could use the bench to peel themselves out of their leather uniform and get back into their civilian clothes—after a shower, of course.

The sounds came louder now. Something wet and squishy. Moans that weren't so much carnal as they were deeply pained. And not necessarily moans that were human in nature. Something about the sounds drew Kyle forth. He couldn't explain it. His search for the ring was futile while the squishy, slurping thing echoed from the next room.

Kyle glanced at an array of black leather masks as he walked through a doorway into the next room: a large enclosure with tile and showerheads adorning the walls to the left and right. In the center of the room was something Kyle couldn't fathom, something that should not be. He wasn't entirely sure what he gazed upon, but he knew it was wrong. Wrong on so many levels.

The thing oozed and squished as it bubbled and undulated in place. Some kind of monster without definition. Something that wasn't patterned from human anatomy as so many monsters were in the movies. No arms or legs, just a vile, cancerous-looking mass. Kyle felt the urge to flee, and yet he felt something else. Something in the low moaning sounds that echoed from the mass, something in the sweet, sticky wetness of the thing reminded him of a familiarity he couldn't quite put his finger on.

Kyle took steps forward and the thing came better into focus. That's when Kyle recognized that it had, indeed, been modeled from human anatomy. Before him was a writhing patchwork of sex organs fused together in angry red flesh. Vaginas that opened and closed like hungry mouths, leaking fluids that dripped onto the ground in a spatter of bloody pus. Air escaped from time to time like juicy queefs, as if there was some kind of pressure from within seeking release, like hydraulics on a city bus. Tufts of hair grew from the mass here and there, like moss on the side of a cliff or roots poking through from trees above. Penises dangled, bobbing as they became engorged and then lost the blood flow. Some lay flaccid like jelly-filled sheaths, as if they did not function properly anymore. Some remained erect, pointing to the ceiling. Some moved around seeming to have a mind of their own, seeking the parted lips of some wandering lover. Puckered assholes across the undulating mass expanded and contracted, several leaking shit.

Kyle took all of this in while his mind screamed at him to go. *Forget the ring!* But there was this deeper part of his mind that fought to keep him planted there. The smell of the thing triggered something that caused a stirring in his pants even as he watched in revulsion as dribbles of semen leaked from the protruding cocks.

Just as Kyle felt he'd gained enough control of his body to turn and flee, the center of the thing began to split, the low moans quivering into something that was an equal measure of ecstasy and agony. Pain and pleasure. The split looked like a large vagina, the inside red and wet. The smell it emitted was both rancid and enticing, like sex and ass, like death and divinity. From within the folds of the split mass, a man emerged, one arm extended. Kyle recognized him as the fellow who'd directed him to the locker room the day before, Assless Chaps. His black hair was slicked back with what must have been a mix of vaginal secretions and cum. His body was red like a fever, like a demon. Eyes wild.

In his outstretched hand was the jewelry box.

The man breathed hard and heavy as if he'd just jogged for miles. His own penis was flaccid but looked angry red like the rest of him. His body had a glistening sheen, and the scent of him was pure sex, with only slight whiffs of foul bodily functions that came from the mass around him.

"You want this?" the man asked, his eyes wide and never closing.

Kyle paused, unsure if the man was referring to the box or . . . the sex pod.

"I just want the ring."

The man nodded, eyes never leaving Kyle's. "But do you want . . . *this*?"

Now Kyle knew he was referring to the thing from which he'd crawled, like a creature from some primordial sex soup.

Kyle forced himself to shake his head even though his loins told him otherwise. It was incredible, the pull the sex pod had on him. It was the smell. It was the sounds. Complete takeover of his senses. A veritable pied piper with a skin flute that played the dulcet sounds of sheer pleasure.

The man stepped out of the fleshy pod completely. Inside, it was red and wet like a womb. Kyle's eyes stared transfixed.

"You want it," the man said.

Kyle shook his head, but words wouldn't come to him.

"You want it. I know you do."

"The ring."

"This?" The man held up the box. "This box or that one, Kyle?"

The man held the jewelry box in front of Kyle's face, outstretched and hovering in the open center of his palm like an offering. Or a test. Kyle went for it, but the man was quicker and tossed the diminutive box into the vaginal-like opening of the flesh pod.

"Get it if you must," the man said.

Kyle didn't hesitate. He reached in, then stepped inside when he realized he couldn't reach the jewelry box now wedged into pink fleshy substance oozing some kind of seminal-like fluids. On stepping into the gaping opening, it promptly closed around him. Kyle was caught like a curious insect in a Venus flytrap.

The man's laughter could be heard from outside, but it was drowned out by the moaning voices that seemed to reverberate from inside the flesh pod. There was movement from within, like muscles flexing, hands grabbing, tearing at Kyle's clothes. His shirt was removed, then his pants.

He held tight to the jewelry box.

His underwear was removed and he could feel something wet slide over his erect penis. He didn't want this, but it felt oh so good. Something like a tight, eager vagina mixed with a talented, toothless mouth. It felt wrong but in such a right way. Try as he might, he couldn't resist the rising vibrations of pleasure that trickled up his body within the all-encompassing warmth of the fleshy thing he'd become absorbed into.

He wouldn't allow the slippery, wet mass to extract the jewelry box from his grasp. When the pleasure became so intense that he knew release was imminent, his hand loosened, but he held tight to the box. It was then, at the precise moment he was going to ejaculate, that the moaning voices changed, taking on a more pained cadence. It was then that the grasp on his raging cock tightened as if squeezing off the urge to cum. It was then that the flesh undulating around him tightened, squeezing the breath from him, causing the panicked feeling of claustrophobia to set in.

Pained cries turned to tearful pleas. Things from within pawed at the jewelry box. Angry things. What had administered the ultimate pleasure moments ago was now as deadly as being trapped inside a jellyfish pod. Stinging erupted and pain radiated throughout his body. He gritted his teeth.

Both hands clasped around the jewelry box, Kyle pried it open and extracted Samantha's ring. He slid it onto one of his fingers, and just as eagerly as the flesh pod had accepted Kyle as a plaything, it rejected him, opening once again and spitting him out onto the tiled floor of the large shower room.

The naked man, who earlier had been so happy within the confines of the flesh pod, stared down at Kyle's labored visage.

"I offered you something so many would give everything for." The man smiled as he shook his head. "You're not supposed to be here. This isn't a place for someone like you. No one has *ever* gone in and come back without total absorption."

Kyle looked up from the chilly tile, with something like afterbirth dripping off him. He felt cold in body and spirit.

The man reached a hand out, then nodded. "You were never meant to be here, and yet you came back. I didn't actually think you'd come back. Who would?"

Kyle didn't take the hand offered to him, wary of the man's touch. He stood up on shaky legs, gathering his discarded clothes that had also been spat out of the fleshy blob, now idle. It had quieted down, but gasses continued escaping as tongues flapped madly across the surface. Kyle didn't look at it directly. He could feel that strange carnal pull and didn't want to become enchanted by the thing.

"Go," the man said, "but don't tell anyone about your experience here. Not what you saw today or yesterday. This place isn't for people like you. And remember, we're everywhere.

We're watching. And despite you not fitting in or accepting my offering, we can always use new meat."

Kyle walked away, not daring to turn his back on the King of the Sadists. Just as he got to the doorway leading into the locker room, he picked up his speed and made his escape. The last thing he heard from behind him was, "We have a mattress waiting for you."

Vengeance of The Donut Man

The day Tim Vance ran out of money was the day he gave his life to The Donut Man.

The Donut Man was an old-school arcade game that happened to be in the corner of Tim's local donut shop next to one of those claw machines filled with cheap stuffed animals that always slipped out of the claw's grasp at the last moment. Kind of a strange amusement for a donut shop, but it was always there, collecting dust.

The Donut Man game made sense. It was as if the game had been made for Rose's Donuts. Tim had seen that arcade game going back to when he was just a little guy carted in there for a sugary breakfast before school, but only on occasion. It was a treat, though more for his mother than himself; she ordering at least three donuts and allowing him only one. He chose the bear claw because it was the largest in the display window. She always grumbled about the price—bear claws cost more than a normal-sized donut—but conceded, and always with a smile, for Wendy Vance's son could do no wrong.

Those donuts caught up to her. Clogged her arteries. A widowmaker heart attack took her away from a young Tim, leaving him alone with his workaholic father. A good man but never around. He used work to battle his demons, to get over losing his wife, never considering that perhaps becoming closer to his son would have been a more viable option to tackle grief.

That was years ago. Tim hadn't ever gotten a job, even after high school. He was the perennial couch potato, only going out to play The Donut Man at Rose's Donuts. Until he finally ran out of money.

Well, finally ran out of his daddy's money. He'd been pilfering loose change from a drawer where his pops kept it when he emptied out his pockets after work. His father always ate fast food on his lunch breaks and always paid with cash, thus always having change. Somehow, the man didn't notice that his change drawer never filled up but was, in fact, nearly empty of anything besides pennies, which Tim never touched, as if he had some kind of physical aversion to them. He'd thought about rolling them so he could exchange the rolls for quarters, but that was too much work.

The reason Tim ran out of what seemed to be an everlasting allowance of spare change was that his father finally began using his debit card for everything. The spare change drawer had become a sea of copper-colored disks bearing the face of President Lincoln. Useless.

The objective of The Donut Man was to complete levels to win each donut until constructing a full donut armor for battle with the final boss, which was a very large, hungry man with chocolate smeared across his mouth like he'd had his tongue crammed up someone's poop chute. With each cruller, glazed, maple bar, and chocolate sprinkle donut acquired, The Donut Man gained strength and new weapons for battle with the hungry idiots intent on eating his donut armor. It was an older game with blocky, pixilated graphics, one that had been a hit with kids back in the day, but now it sat under a blanket of dusty spiderwebs, a forgotten timepiece in the annals of pop culture history.

Tim had begun playing the game religiously after his mother passed. He remembered seeing it all those years ago when they would go to Rose's Donuts for breakfast. He'd asked to play, and she would always scoff and tell him it was an insult to heavyset people, being that the enemies in the game were grotesquely overweight. Tim hadn't understood, but he accepted her reasoning.

Tim spent his last two quarters only making it to the third boss before his fried pastry armor had been consumed, which caused his body to spontaneously sink into a bubbling vat of frying oil and shrink to a crispy black stick figure, and GAME

OVER flashed in bloody red raspberry jam dotted with tiny seeds for the last time.

Tim stared at it for a while before he realized he was crying.

"What are you doing?" a voice asked. It was Dennis, the old man who owned and ran the donut shop with his wife, Sue. They worked there every day of their life as if they were shackled to the place. They had family members who worked there, too, but Dennis and Sue were helplessly devoted to donuts as a passion before a business. They had always been friendly and nice going back to when Tim was a child. Dennis used to give Tim a sort of crooked smile when his mother wasn't looking and give him a free donut hole.

Tim craned his head to see the man standing behind the glass display case, a quizzical look on his face.

"What are you doing over there?" Dennis asked, a look of frustration and concern clouding his face.

Tim opened his mouth to say something, but all he could do was blubber. He was in a bad place just then. He was lost.

Dennis shook his head. "I don't understand. You come in here every day like clockwork. You buy three or four donuts. You stare at that damn video game. Hasn't worked in six, seven years at least. You leave. Don't say anything but your order. Pay with spare change." Dennis shook his head. "Now this? What gives?"

After staring at one another for maybe thirty seconds, Tim offered Dennis that mischievous grin they used to share. Dennis squinted his eyes even more as if either not recognizing or remembering that look. Tim, a large man due to genes and a poor diet, leapt upon the arcade console, wrapping his arms around it and slamming his gut on the shelf with the joystick and buttons, all covered in layers of dust from years of neglect. He sank down onto the machine, one of the joysticks jabbing into his navel.

"Get away from there," Dennis said. He made a move forward, then thought better of it, as he didn't know what to expect from the weirdo who'd managed to heap his girth upon the old game console. Sue put a hand on Dennis's shoulder as if to steady him.

She said to Tim, "Please just go. And get some help."

The worry in her eyes was lost on Tim as he ignored their pleas, grunting as his body threatened to slide off the console or maybe take the thing down with him. His gesticulations were almost carnal in their blubbery renderings.

Tim sobbed as the joystick eased into his belly button like a probing snake, like an eager cock entering a warm hole. Tim's body shuddered as the joystick pushed through the taut flesh of his gut, entering his body. At first, there was a pinch of pain, a little blood that trickled down the shaft of the joystick, trailing onto the circuit board beneath the veneer of the console. The pain radiated into a comforting warmth that enveloped Tim from the inside out.

The joystick undulated, swirling and spinning within Tim's body like the agitator in a washing machine. The warm, soothing feeling caused him to become sick as his gorge rose. The pleasurable sensations turned inward, and it felt as if his guts would open up and release his steaming insides all over the floor of the donut shop. Like some macabre offering to Dennis and Sue, God bless their souls.

"Jesus," came a voice from far off. Could have been either Dennis or Sue, Tim couldn't tell. As panic rose within, it felt like he could hear the blood flowing through his arteries.

Tim puked up a thick batter of undigested donut, sprinkles still visible in the mess that ran down the front of The Donut Man arcade game. The joystick played with his intestines, and then the feeling, which had been undesirable and frightening, became ecstatic. Tim raised his head to face the ceiling, slimy donut juice sliding down his chin. The joystick spun his insides like churning his belly batter into butter.

Tim's eyes opened. The pupils were pixilated squares.

"Call the police," Dennis said. He couldn't take his eyes off Tim.

Tim turned his head toward the donut shop owners. "No!" he said.

Dennis and Sue stared ahead, eyes wide, mouths agape.

Tim stepped back from the machine, the joystick sliding out of the hole in his stomach. Two lengths of intestine snaked out of his guts and hovered over the *A* and *B* buttons beside the joystick, which was gripped tightly with another length of entrails.

Blood seeped from his open wound, saturating his shorts like he'd pissed himself.

"No cops," Tim said. His bowels began moving the joystick and tapping the buttons. "Cops eat donuts."

Tim reached a hand out, fingers splayed. His guts maneuvered the joystick. From within the glass display case not far from where Dennis and Sue stood, a jelly-filled donut sprang to action, twitching and dancing in place. Sue noticed and pointed it out to Dennis. The jelly donut rose and then shot through the glass like a bullet, flinging itself toward Tim, who grabbed it out of the air, a smile spreading across his face. He shoved it right into the bloody hole in his stomach, nestling it within the guts hanging out of the angry wound and controlling the video game.

Sue dropped her cell phone. She bent down to grab it, but when she came up, she had to duck to avoid getting smacked in the face with a jelly-filled donut that was launched at her from across the store. Another jam rocket was flung from Tim's hand, his fingers dripping with gooey, pixilated raspberry filling.

Wet intestine flicked the joystick left and right as another purple rope of innards slapped the *A* and *B* buttons. Through the sheen of puke, the screen of The Donut Man game came to life. On it was the front counter of Rose's Donuts with Dennis and Sue as NPCs in pixilated brilliance. Non-Playable Characters. Limited in their movements. Controlled by the program.

Dennis and Sue stood behind the counter stiff and straight, their eyes reflecting the fear of their sudden immobility.

"What is going on?" Sue asked, her voice coming out in choppy syllables, mouth opening and closing robotically.

"I do not know," Dennis replied, his gestures identical to his wife's.

Both Dennis and Sue began moving left to right behind the display case, continuing to stand straight up, facing forward. Only their eyes darted around as if trapped within bodies that were under a spell.

As Tim's character on the video game screen launched jelly donut discs at Dennis and Sue, he launched the same from his drippy hand. One just missed Dennis, who dropped down like he was a living embodiment of Whac-A-Mole. Sue, on the other hand, was hit in the face. She screamed, the acid-like jam within the pastry having seared off her skin, revealing some of her skull through the sticky melted-off flesh that dripped from her face in thick chunks.

A maple bar leapt out of the case and directly into Tim's exposed gut. A power up chime erupted through the donut shop speakers that usually played oldies.

Dennis was back at attention. "This hurts," he said. "My body aches."

A sort of sob came out of Sue's throat. Dennis robotically turned his head to see that half of his wife's face was gone. The edges were pixilated, and the skull poking through had a square hollow for the eye. But she was somehow still alive.

Dennis and Sue began moving left and right again, ducking from time to time, then back up. A mechanical dance that moved their bodies in ways they never had before, even in their younger days.

Tim's hand changed from dripping red jelly to a coating of maple glaze. Out of nowhere, he produced a maple bar with razor-sharp blades extending from both ends. When Tim threw the donut at Dennis and Sue, three of them flung out, spinning and deadly. Sue was hit in the throat, the lethal pastry decapitating her in a gush of blood that sprayed from the stump as a geyser with enough force to reach the ceiling. Another spinning maple bar hit Dennis, embedding in his chest. His eyes and teeth clamped shut from the impact.

"Level up!" a robotic voice said through the shop speakers.

A glazed and a powdered donut sprang forth from the display, flew across the shop, and safely deposited within Tim's torn gut. His intestines continued maneuvering the joystick and tapping the A and B buttons. His body began to gloss over with a sheen of glazing as his donut armor took shape. Muscles formed all shiny and tanned, like glazed twists.

"One more hit and I beat the level," Tim said as Dennis shifted left and right, ducking here and there, his face pained and frightened. He moved quicker, making him a more challenging target.

SICK! SICK! SICK!

"Don't. Do this," Dennis said.

Tim threw a powdered donut at Dennis. When the pastry hit the counter, it exploded into a burst of powdery smoke, immobilizing Dennis, who stood there staring at his adversary, completely covered in powdered sugar but unable to move. His eyes went wide as Dennis threw one of the glazed donuts at him. It landed, adhering to him by the gummy glazing. The donut ticked. Ticked. Ticked. And then the pastry grenade exploded, blowing Dennis's body apart in a wash of blood and guts. His pixilated insides decorated Rose's Donuts. Bones, blood, organs, and brains slid down the walls and countertops, dripping from the ceiling.

For completing the level, Tim was awarded a bag of donut holes.

The screen on the video game changed to show a police cruiser pulling into the parking lot, as one did exactly that in reality. The cop stepped out of the cruiser, a large man who looked winded just standing up. He opened the back door and out came his partner, a German Shepherd.

As soon as the door opened and the cop walked in, Tim launched one of the bladed maple bars, but the cop was quick for his size and ducked it. Tim threw his last jelly-filled, hitting the officer's arm in a splat of raspberry acid. As the officer pulled his firearm, Tim lobbed one of the powdered donut immobilization bombs. The German Shepherd was ahead of the explosion, unaffected by the powder, which left the officer stunned.

In a quick movement by his controlling intestines, Tim threw another glazed sticky grenade at the cop, then reached into the bag of donut holes, throwing one in front of the German Shepherd. When the donut hole hit the ground, it created a black void, but the dog jumped it. Just as the dog hopped, the grenade exploded, launching pieces of the cop in every direction like human confetti, punctuated by a power up chime from the donut shop speakers.

Tim's guts shifted the joystick and tapped the buttons, but the K-9 was quick, evading another bladed maple bar and leaping through a final cloud of immobilization powder as it reached The Donut Man, obese with muscles glistening with sticky icing. The dog growled and barked and went right for his sweet center, the gaping gut hole filled with gloriously delectable donut offerings. The dog pulled out the pastries, gobbling them up one by one. As Tim's powers decreased, his muscles deflated as the glazing dried up. Once the donuts were gone, the pup chewed the lengths of intestine that tethered Tim to the game.

From the speakers came the downbeat notes of losing that were always accompanied by two words: GAME OVER, as raspberry jelly oozed out of The Donut Man's gaping stomach cavity.

Beneath Tim, a pit of roiling fryer grease opened up and he sank into its depths, skin crisping, then cracking as his insides swelled and expanded from the heat, exiting out his torn stomach. As his flesh turned to cracklings and chunks of fat melted into the searing oil, all that was left were his blackened bones.

My 6000 Pound Wife

I woke up this morning, looked at the woman beside me in bed and thought, *Is it me, or has she gained some weight?* A strange thought first thing in the morning, yes, but that was my observation.

How did we get here? When you live with someone, you don't notice those little changes, even the big ones. Weight, wrinkles, and even gray hairs sneak up on you. They snuck up on me, the wrinkles at least. I don't really notice them until I sit in the den after Maddie goes to sleep and I take up my pipe. The weed sets in and I feel fuzzy, then end up in the bathroom looking at myself real close. That's when *I* see the wrinkles.

I'm not so sure Maddie sees her weight, and I am certainly not saying anything to her about it. I know better. But as I look at her bulk while fighting the seasick sensation that I am going to roll into her by the very pull her struggling side of the bed has on me, I wonder if it is my obligation to say something.

For her health.

For our relationship.

Because I'll be goddamned, but it looks like she gained weight overnight.

I slipped out of bed unnoticed, which wasn't hard. Somehow, Maddie didn't have sleep apnea and managed to sleep like she fell into a coma every night. At the doorway, I turned for another look. The bed was crooked and that wasn't right. Had it been that way when I went to sleep last night? How did I not roll right into her? The comforter looked like a baby blanket draped over her swollen body.

As I stumbled sleepily down the hallway, I wondered if I had some kind of dream-induced hallucination. It didn't make sense. Bodies don't grow that fast. It takes time to put on fat, just like it takes time to tone muscle.

When you don't see someone in a good while, they can change, and then it's really noticeable. I see Maddie every day, so her changes sneak up on me. She'd gotten quite large at one time, but a strict diet and exercise regimen got her back to a somewhat respectable weight. Some people say big is beautiful, but it's not about the beauty. It's about health. I want my Maddie to live as long as possible. I want us to grow old together.

As coffee percolated, I thought about what I'd woken up to. Yep, must have been a dream lingering from my mind into the waking world. Once Maddie wakes up, she'll come out of the bedroom as normal as can be.

"Rod?"

Oh, she's awake.

"Yes," I called back, waiting for the final drop of coffee to seep through the grounds.

"Could you give me some help here?"

Help? Help for what?

"Uh, just a moment, dear."

I thought I heard her groan (or was that the bed?), but couldn't be sure. Once I had my coffee, I felt much better. I've always denied that coffee is a drug, but it sure did open my eyes every morning.

Once I got back into our room, my eyes opened even wider. Maddie was larger now. The size of the entire king-sized bed.

"I don't know if I can get out of bed today," she said.

I almost dropped my coffee in dramatic fashion, just like in the movies, but I steadied myself and took another drink, silent in the presence of a bastard miracle. Yes, miracle. They aren't all for good, you know.

"What are you staring at?" she asked.

I swallowed hard, still unsure what to think, much less say to her in that moment.

"What, are you just gonna stand there and stare, or are you gonna help me?" she asked.

"Help you, dear." The words came out almost robotically, for I had no idea what I was supposed to do to help. She didn't look like she could get out of bed if she wanted to. And what was I to do? I'm not exactly a muscular man.

SICK! SICK! SICK!

"I just want to scoot up a bit so I can see the TV better. Can you help me?"

She started shifting her weight left and right as if trying to squirm herself into a more upright position. I leapt across the floor to the quivering bed, her motions inching the frame to and fro, the feet scratching the hardwood with irreparable divots. I grabbed an arm, hoping to steady her and do what I could to assist. It was like grabbing a big ol' water balloon filled with Jell-O. I couldn't get a good grip, but I kind of hugged her thick arm and did my best to pull her up and back.

It was all so exhausting, but she somehow settled into a better position. She inhaled and exhaled heavily like a woman in labor. The very action of merely breathing caused the bed to whimper.

"Feed me," Maddie said.

My mind went blank. It was a demand, "Feed me." Like the plant in *Little Shop of Horrors*.

Her voice was becoming whiny. "Rod, feed me."

"What would you like, dear?"

"Bacon, eggs, toast, potatoes, Pop-Tarts, hash browns, and bacon. Extra butter. Lotsa salt."

What kind of breakfast order was that?

"Uh, honey, are you . . . feeling all right?"

She grabbed the remote with a hand so thick and puffy you'd have thought she'd been stung by a bee. After turning on the TV, her head pivoted on a neck like folds of pink rubber. Her eyes seemed beadier than before. She breathed with her mouth open, making nauseating sounds as each struggled breath fought its way from her lungs and out of her mouth.

"I'd be feeling a lot better if you'd feed me."

I merely nodded and walked out of the room. I didn't know what to say. I felt like I was in a nightmare, but conscious of it. The horror wouldn't end. In the kitchen, I searched for the ingredients to make breakfast. No, I wasn't about to make two forms of potatoes and extra bacon. Just a normal breakfast. I was certain when I arrived back in the bedroom that she would be the same Maddie I went to sleep next to last night. This had to be some kind of bizarre hallucination.

As I was cooking, I realized I hadn't seen the dog all morning. "Charlie? Charlie-boy?"

Bacon sizzled as homestyle potatoes cooked. Charlie was nowhere to be found, which was unusual, considering he was a total beggar and loitered around my feet whenever I was in the kitchen, hoping for a scrap to fall.

I walked into the bedroom, the words dying on my lips at what I saw. "Maddie, have you seen—"

She'd dwarfed the bed. And I mean, she was as big as the fucking room. Her body lay in a heap where there once was a bed. Her head was about touching the ceiling. Her feet had smashed into the dresser—now precariously leaning against the wall—that held the TV.

"Have I seen what?" she asked, as if nothing was out of the ordinary.

Again, I was frozen. How the hell was this happening, and why was it happening to me?

"The . . . the dog." And then I called for him. "Charlie?"

I heard a muffled bark, then whimpering coming from somewhere to the left of Maddie's girth.

"Charlie-boy? Where are you? Charlie?"

Another muffled bark or two and that whimpering. It was coming from Maddie's flabby thigh, crisscrossed with varicose veins and stretch marks that looked like mountain ranges on the map of her flesh. I looked closely and saw Charlie's leg and tail crushed beneath the avalanche of fat.

"Oh shit! Charlie!"

I grabbed his leg and gently tugged, but he was in there pretty good and probably struggling to breathe. I grabbed hold of her thigh meat as well as I could and lifted.

"Come on, Charlie!"

"What are you doing?" Maddie asked. "Bacon's burning! I can smell it."

I ignored her, lifting her jellified thigh as much as I could until Charlie had enough room to squeeze out. The little terrier mix freed himself and ran out of the room.

"Get the darned bacon!" Maddie yelled.

"You were sitting on the fucking dog?"

She glowered at me. "Language!"

I bowed my head. I'd curse with the boys at work before I retired, but I never brought that kind of talk home. At least not unless I was really angry, which I kind of was in that moment.

"I'll get the bacon," I said, and left the room.

Poor Charlie was lapping up water like he'd been confined for days without it. I'm just glad he was okay. For a second there, I thought . . . No, no, no, I couldn't think that way about Maddie. Not my sweet Maddie. She'd never . . . Or would she?

I brought the food and wasn't nearly as shocked as I should have been when I couldn't get into the damn room because her girth had ballooned to the point of filling it. She was yelling for food, but her voice sounded distant because her head had expanded through the ceiling and into the attic.

I went into the garage and pulled down the attic stairs, deciding to bring the food up to her. It actually worked out pretty well this way. Her head had burst through broken hunks of drywall between two joists. I stood over her upturned face and slid over-easy eggs right into her mouth. It was vile work. She sucked the slimy eggs down like a goddamned garbage disposal. She didn't even chew, just slurped them whole, bits of yolk popping up sometimes like a yellow geyser. She chomped the bacon and didn't even complain that half of it was burnt. Next came the potatoes. At this point, I was so disgusted with the whole ordeal that I tilted the plate and funneled them in.

Nom nom nom nom nom!

I recoiled as my gorge rose, acidic coffee threatening to spew forth. I held it down but wasn't entirely sure she would have been averse to consuming my vomit, the very thought of which caused my stomach to roil.

After the toast was snatched out of my hand by her clenching teeth, munched, and swallowed into the black hole of her throat, she panted, food bits clinging to the folds of her cheek and neck like a toddler after a meal.

"That's it?"

"That was enough for two of us," I said.

"No hash browns?"

The smell that came out of the face protruding through the attic floor was equal parts breakfast buffet and bad breath. I started feeling lightheaded. As I stepped down the stairs, she called out to me, "Feed me. Feed me! FEED ME!"

I left the house and took Charlie with me. I didn't know what else to do. I wanted to leave and never come back, but I couldn't do that to Maddie. We'd been together for so many years. I loved the woman dearly but hated seeing what was happening to her— especially at such a rapid rate. I felt as if I didn't even know her anymore.

By the time my mind cleared, I realized I was hungry. I'd skipped out on breakfast and lost my appetite after feeding it all to Maddie. Thinking about it made me queasy. I stopped in at a fast-food joint and ordered a hamburger and fries. It would be lunchtime when I got home, so I decided to get Maddie something. Question was, what would she like? Or better yet, how *much* would she like?

I settled on ten burgers and five orders of fries. Even that didn't seem like enough, but it was costly. And it just didn't seem right to order more.

When Charlie and I got home, I thought there was something different about the house. Something was off. It seemed as if the framing had shifted somehow. Then I saw that a couple of the windows were cracked. There were fissures running along the stucco that had not been there before.

When I tried to open the door, it wouldn't budge. It was jammed. I gave it a good push and finally freed it from the tight compression of the frame, a sure result of the structural damage I could see from the outside. What I faced upon entering was so shocking that I dropped both bags of food on the floor. Charlie was also terrified, but not so much that he could resist digging his face into the fallen bag of burgers.

Maddie had grown so huge that she took up nearly the entire interior of the house. She completely demolished the ceiling and walls, causing the attic rafters to become visible from the foyer, and she dwarfed most everything in the house except for a small portion of the entrance. Her gelatinous body was marred with weeping gashes from the broken framework, lacerations so big they spilled buckets of blood, but none of that seemed to bother her.

"Feed me!" her voice boomed.

"I brought you food," I said, then looked down to see Charlie amid a pile of wrappers.

Maddie grimaced and it was one of the worst things I've ever seen. Pure hatred.

From her bulging stomach, which took up every inch of the living room, thick stretch marks lined her belly vertically. One of them in the center that lined up with her cavern of a belly button, began to split like overripe fruit. The split was red and wet as the halves of her gut peeled away to expose her steamy insides, blood trickling down to the rancid cleft of her vagina, tangled in a network of thick hair like the roots of an old tree.

"I'm hungry, Rod. Feed me. Feed me directly."

I shook my head and took a step back toward the door.

Maddie's breathing increased, causing gusts of hot air that smelled of halitosis and vomit.

"Then I'll feed myself!" she said as thick blue ropes of intestine emerged from her wet guts, lurching forth and snatching Charlie off the floor. The dog yelped as it was carried into the air and drawn into the massive woman's guts, its whimpering and screeching barks silenced as Maddie's insides tightened around the animal like a boa constrictor on a mouse.

Her stomach sealed up, leaving a red seam down the center where the stretch mark had split open like a new mouth, now closed after a satisfying meal.

"Now you!" Maddie said as she reached out her massive hand and grabbed me.

I hadn't been prepared to run. I didn't see this coming. She grabbed me like a doll, wrapping her fat digits around me. I squirmed, but it was no use. She had a good grip on my legs.

"You haven't given Momma what she likes in such a long time, Rodney."

At first, I flailed, then soon realized there was nothing I could do at the mercy of this hulking giant.

"Please stop!" I yelled, but my voice was so weak in contrast to hers. And that look in her eyes. It was like she was going to eat me like a grilled chicken leg.

But that's not what Momma wanted.

She shifted her body, which caused the framework to groan in protest, windows shattering, joists bending, but she managed to get herself into a position she liked by thrusting her massive pelvis up a bit. And God help me, that's when I realized what she had in mind for me.

"Give Momma some sugar," she said, and then she used my entire body like a sex toy and jammed me up inside of her.

On impact, I saw the thick, ropy hair, like vines hanging off a freeway overpass, and then total darkness. Moist darkness. Like wading in the juicy bottom of a garbage bin at the dock where the fishermen cast off the remains of their catch. Whereas earlier I had managed not to puke into her mouth while feeding her in the attic, I couldn't hold back my lunch and puked into the vaginal void.

She thrust my body in and out and no matter what I did, no matter how much I flailed my arms or grabbed onto a handful of ropelike hairs, nothing perturbed her until she was finished.

I was extracted and left in the foyer of the house in a heaping puddle of vomit and rank fluids. Maddie was breathing hard, but the noxious fumes from her gullet weren't nearly as bad as what I'd just been subjected to. Then, her stomach didn't merely growl but more or less rumbled to the extent that it was probably detected on the Richter scale.

I knew what that meant.

I scrambled to right myself, slipping on the vaginal fluids and vomit that my entire body was steeped in. Somehow, after my return, the front door had been closed. There wasn't much space in the house between me and the all-encompassing girth of Maddie.

Her stomach cracked like booming thunder. She said, "Uh oh," and then it happened.

The smell hit me first. The worst diarrhea ever. My reflex was to gag and puke, and that's why my mouth was open when the tidal wave of liquid shit hit me like a breaker on a beach. I continued to scramble to get to the front door, but it was no use. The valve had been opened. Liquid shit filled the remaining space of the house, only spilling out when it reached the broken windows. Chunks of half-digested food clung to my body like debris in a storm drain.

I tried to get out, but I had become sucked into the maelstrom and, thus, drowned in the molten feces of my six-thousand-pound wife.

Blood Expectations

Nurses are known as kind and helping individuals, but you'd be surprised how many of them are absolutely crazy motherfuckers.

Take my pal, Andre. He went through nursing school right out of high school and for all the wrong reasons. What are the wrong reasons, you ask? Well, he wanted to learn as much as he could about keeping people alive without going through all the schooling to become a doctor. He didn't have the brains to be a doctor anyhow. We used to fantasize about killing people. How we would do it. What we would use for a murder weapon. Something different than what you see in movies. Something cool. Andre was fascinated with suffering, kind of like Pinhead.

I think he got into the medical field to learn how to make people suffer.

But what he did with that knowledge was even worse, for weird ethical reasons that I feel deep down but don't even really understand myself. Andre and I, we were birthed—not merely cut—from the same bolt of cloth, in a way. "Brothers from another mother," we used to say. Two guys fascinated with the fantasy of murder? Well, that was some real Henry Lee Lucas and Ottis Toole shit. Most teenagers were off partying or screwing around while we were reading up on serial killers and plotting some really nasty shit. We almost went through with some of it too. But you know what they say, "Dead men tell no tales." We'd have ended up killing each other out of sheer paranoia and we both knew it.

Ours was a rare friendship that lasted after high school when many others drifted apart, going off to college or getting married and living that white picket fence life. Andre and I, we lived together in an apartment. Started partying hard, bringing girls back and taking turns with them if they were so inclined. Drugs and alcohol made panties fall off. It was fun, but something was lacking. Maybe married life called to us. Maybe we were missing out. Andre was going to nursing school at the time. That's how he found access to good, clean drugs. But, alas, the fun never lasts, and I met a woman and eventually moved out. However, white picket fences were not in my future.

I got the call from Andre a couple of days before we ventured out to this cabin he bought. Crazy son of a bitch. I'd signed divorce papers that morning. Called Andre and told him I wanted to party, just to shake it all off and forget. Married life, as it turned out, wasn't for me. My urges lay elsewhere, and my wife didn't understand. I loved Brittany, but she was far too vanilla. It wasn't just the sex, but everything. The finality of settling down bored me. When I talked of the things me and Andre used to talk about, she clammed up. Sometimes she looked fearful.

For instance, I told her about how I wanted to wrap someone's arm in a tourniquet and inject lemon juice into their veins, just to see what would happen when I pulled the tourniquet free. The worry in her eyes at that comment . . . Another time, I told her how I would love to anesthetize someone's hands and flay the flesh and muscle off their fingers, leaving bones jutting. Just to see how long someone could live like that. How they could function. Brittany didn't talk to me for the rest of the night.

I couldn't be with someone like that. It wasn't as if I was going to act out these fantasies. They were just imaginings. Thing was, her revulsion turned me on, so I pushed and I pushed, coming up with the most vile tortures to the human body I could think up. Force-feeding a man his own shit. Inserting a feeding tube from stomach to mouth just to see how long it would take for the cycle of stomach acid to eat through the tender flesh of the throat and mouth. Stitching a woman from vagina to asshole (and adding superglue for a good seal) just to observe the ramifications of a body that could not relieve itself.

Brittany became so disgusted with my fantasies that she filed for divorce. These were thoughts Andre and I had discussed time and again, sober or fucked up. Maybe I was foolish to think that other people could share such wondrous visions. Maybe

Andre and I were meant to be together. Not in a sexual way, but in some deeper way.

I'd been talking to Andre a lot in the weeks that led up to my inevitable divorce. I'd moved out of the house into a shitty little apartment in a run-down building above a long abandoned market. I'd begun to fantasize about what I could do with such a space as that below my apartment.

When Andre called about the cabin, I knew why he'd wanted me up there.

Only I didn't know at all.

All smiles and tittering on the ride up, I was sure he was going to surprise me. I confess I was giddy at the prospect. After reading book after book about serial killers and what makes them tick, I was sure the introduction to that vile game would be the first domino in a bastard series that would be the cause of much suffering and pain. I also knew incarceration would likely be the end result, but at that moment I was hurting inside. The hurting made me want to act out every sick fantasy I'd ever had. I was ready to open the gates.

But what he showed me in the cabin threw me for a loop.

After Andre unlocked no less than five deadbolts, we entered. He punched in a code for an alarm system, turned to me, and his smile couldn't have been more broad, for the cabin was essentially one large room with a loft above, and chained to a bed up against the back wall was . . .

"Ain't she a beaut?" he asked.

Standing there in the doorway, I was shocked into silence. "What the hell is that?"

"Come inside," Andre urged. "Close the door. You're letting the cold in. Get over here and have a closer look."

After a moment of hesitation, a feeling of reserve came over me, a feeling that I should flee, but where could I go? I entered and closed the door. As I approached the bed on the other side of the cabin, the thing came into better focus. It was human in form but hairy all over. Its eyes were closed, but I could see the steady rise and fall of its breasts and knew it was alive and breathing. Its face was hardly feminine, surrounded by coarse hair, with ears protruding from the sides like dried fruit. The breasts were engorged, the flesh dark as if deeply tanned. Hair covered the majority of its body, only exposing the palms of her hands and feet, her face, and chest. Her stomach, which bulged, was dusted in a lighter covering of hair than the rest of her body.

"Haven't figured it out?" Andre asked.

All I could do was shake my head.

"She's a fucking Sasquatch, man."

"What?"

"A Sas—"

"I know what you said. I mean, what the fuck?"

It was then that I saw the contraption he devised. Her arms were shackled with chains that were fastened to the floor through the loops of giant, sturdy bolts. Her ankles were also shackled, though the chains were attached to a series of pulleys also fastened to the floor, then probably driven deep down into a concrete slab beneath the floorboards.

"I know what you're thinking," he said. "She isn't going anywhere."

"Actually, I was thinking you're a fucking nutjob."

Andre laughed. "Dude, this is fucking amazing, okay. I mean seriously. It seems kind of gross at first, but just you wait and see."

"Gross?"

Andre nodded. "Yeah. Fucking her."

"You . . . ?"

"Don't knock it till you try it. Seriously."

My eyes kept going back to the bulging stomach.

"I know, I know," he continued, "the Depends aren't the most sexy thing in the world. I have to put them on her, or she'll shit the bed. I mean, I come out here just about every night to check up on her. To . . . nurse her, if you will. I got all this great stuff from the medical supply warehouse. An IV drip, heart rate monitor, the whole setup. And best of all, I have everything hooked up to a computer that sends the info to an app." Andre could see the trepidation in my eyes. He lowered his voice, taming his excitement. "Look, man, this might seem real far out there, but I'm telling you,"—he leaned in—"this thing gives the best fuck you ever had. I mean, really, dude. See, she starts clenching up. You know what I'm saying?" A sardonic grin. "And holy shit, it's amazing. It's like she's got a goddamned hand in there squeezing tight, but not *too* tight."

I was stunned into silence. This was not at all what I had expected. I'd even brought a special knife with me, one that I'd been holding onto for years, just in case the urge swept over me and I felt the need to take a life. It was the knife I had imagined using on people when we would fantasize about murder.

I wasn't expecting *this*.

Andre pulled off the adult diaper. The smell was revolting.

"Just gotta clean her up a bit and she's ready to go."

Tossing the dirty diaper into a garbage can, he opened a cabinet in the kitchen. Within, the shelves were lined with an entire fucking pharmacy of medications.

"Maybe you want something to relax a bit? You're tense."

I shook my head. "No."

"Sure?" He grabbed a bottle and popped two pills, following it with a swig of beer.

He'd been popping pills all day. I could tell. He was probably numbing his mind from the sick shit he was involved with. I'd come here ready to murder someone, so I suppose I was no better. But seeing this ape-woman chained to the bed really sickened me. Deeply. For some reason, killing a human suited me just fine, or at least I thought it did. I hadn't actually gone through with it yet. But seeing this helpless creature struck a nerve. Humans were trash. People disgusted me. The thing on the bed was an animal. As far as I could see, Andre was fucking an animal. He was into goddamned bestiality!

"How long have you had her here?" I asked.

"Oh, the better part of a year."

"For fuck's sake, Andre, she's pregnant!"

He looked upon the Sasquatch woman with glassy eyes. The slackness of his face attested to how loaded he was. How the hell was he working at the hospital in such a state and managing to come out here every night to keep this creature alive for his own sick pleasure?

Andre shrugged. "Oh well, I guess you're probably right." Then he laughed. "Wonder who the little son of a bitch is gonna look like? Think it'll come out with a lot of hair?"

That joke broke him into a fit of laughter, but I remained stoic. I touched the hilt of the knife I'd brought with me, buckled to my belt in a leather sheath. I realized that I wasn't so sure I could commit murder. Fantasy was one thing. Acting out those fantasies was something else altogether, and here Andre had been acting out some fantasy I had no idea he harbored in that twisted mind of his.

Using a wet rag, he cleaned the Sasquatch's pubis, which woke her. She made a grunt of surprise, but it was very tame compared to what I expected. I suppose after a year of abuse, she had resigned herself to the awful duty and was too weak and exhausted to fight Andre off night after night.

SICK! SICK! SICK!

I stood there not knowing what to do, wanting to be excused from such depravity. I felt a sudden shame for the sick things we used to talk about, for my acceptance of murder for sport, for what I had come up here to do. In that moment, I hated myself the most.

Andre cranked a lever on the pulley system connected to the chains shackled to her ankles, which began pulling her legs spread-eagle. She groaned as he did this. It was a low sound from deep in her throat, an agonized sound because she knew what was to come and she loathed it. It was a pained groan and it made my heart ache.

"I want you to have a go first," Andre said as he finished cranking his pulley contraption. He flashed a toothy smile. "But if you're too much of a pussy, I'll gladly have all the fun myself."

Now that the thing's legs were spread apart, it was clear just how pregnant she was. The fact that Andre raped this creature was vile enough, but that he'd impregnated her and continued violating her like this was too much for me to bear. Something had to be done.

"For fuck's sake, Andre. What the fuck is wrong with you?"

This took him by surprise. He wavered on his feet, high as the night sky on who-knows-what cocktail of pharmaceutical drugs.

"Look at her!" I said. "She's dilating. *You're* the fucking nurse, can't you see that?"

Stepping up to the creature on the bed, Andre had a closer look. At some point, he'd taken his pants off and was stroking himself. *You sick fuck, you!* I grabbed the knife. I'd bought it at a liquor store when I was fifteen, right out of a glass case that sold everything from meth pipes to brass knuckles. It was sharp enough to split hairs and had been waiting to split flesh for many, many years.

Just as Andre was preparing to enter the Sasquatch, he mumbled something about not giving a fuck. That's when I grabbed him by the hair and flung him backward onto the hardwood. He gasped for air and was completely disoriented. I took my knife and stabbed him in each eye, but not deep enough to drive the blade into his brain. Well, not far into his brain. The eyes sort of popped, leaking blood and ocular fluid down his face, which swung back and forth as he tried to escape. I used the blade and whacked his hands away from me, driving deep gashes into the flesh, which opened up bright and red like the petals of a budding rose. In my anger, I kicked his arms, breaking a bone or two and sending them up around his head akimbo, useless. Andre screamed, and from behind me, I heard the Sasquatch roaring.

But I wasn't finished with Andre just yet. I stuck my knife in just above his flaccid penis and dragged it upward, cutting through soft flesh like butter. As his gut opened, his entrails spilled forth as if they had been under pressure. The knife hit the rib cage and stopped. I let go and stood up.

Andre was dead. Blood spilled from his body, cascading across the hardwood, dripping through any groove it accosted until he'd finally bled out, body still, the gamy smell of his innards encompassing me.

The groans and screams from the creature intensified. I turned to see the baby crowning.

"Oh fuck!"

I panicked. Didn't know what to do.

The Sasquatch pushed, driven by the same primordial instinct that any mammal taps into during childbirth. Once the head was out enough for me to grab, I did what felt natural and assisted by gently pulling the baby free from its mother's womb. The placenta followed, after which a gush of dark blood poured forth onto the bed. The poor creature took a few gasping breaths and then she was quiet. I knew that she'd died.

The baby wailed.

Again, I panicked. *What the fuck is going on?*

I grabbed a towel from the kitchen area and patted the slimy afterbirth off the tiny creature. It had, indeed, been born with lots of hair, as Andre had joked. I looked the thing in the face but couldn't see any obvious relation to Andre. It had to be his, though, if he'd held this female Sasquatch here for over a year, and assuming Sasquatch have a similar gestation period as humans.

I panicked. Nothing had gone the way I'd expected, and there I was, holding some weird hybrid baby. While I was pacing the room and gathering my thoughts, I slipped on Andre's blood. Shifting my weight to avoid falling, I flung my body forward and slipped even more, instinctually putting my hands out to break my fall. I went down hard, the newborn hybrid beneath me. It yelped and then was silent. I clambered up and saw that the soft tissue of its head—what hadn't developed into skull yet—had ruptured, leaking blood and gooey ropes of brain, looking like custard that had turned.

Where there were four of us, there's now just one.

That's my story. That's what happened. That's the God's honest truth.

I took Andre's car. Had to. Couldn't walk all that way. I drove away thinking about how it wasn't like what I had anticipated. Feeling disappointed and unfulfilled, I decided to give my ex a visit. For once, I figured she would meet my expectations.

Blowout

Todd Wagner couldn't be more excited to be invited to a Blowout party. He'd heard of Blowouts, but they were pretty much exclusively invite-only. "It's who you know and who you blow." He just figured he wasn't blowing the right men.

Four lines of speed were chopped out on a square mirror, waiting to be inhaled via reddened nostrils. Todd had been using speed for a few years now. He started back in his senior year of high school as a way to escape from what, at the time, was proving to be not only a stressful life but one of shame and frustration. It hadn't been easy coming out of the closet, so it was a surprise that most of his friends and schoolmates had already suspected him of being queer. Sort of explained why he was bullied so much. Some people just couldn't get into the twenty-first century and still, like their degenerate parents had done, found superiority in picking on people who were different from them.

It was Todd's best friend, Chloe, who turned him on to speed. She was a Goth chick who liked to wear torn fishnet stockings and black lipstick. She was beating a dead horse carrying an image that died along with Marilyn Manson's career, but it was her thing. And so was meth.

Todd took to meth like a lit match to dusty drapes. He found solace and comfort in the high. A bonus side effect was that he had the energy of four men and could get his schoolwork done in record time. But the best part about speed was what he and his first boyfriend, Jared Greenhorn, discovered. It was a hell of an aphrodisiac, and with the stamina of four men, he could fuck all night long. At least until his dick got sore, and the meth had a way of covering up things like that. He once fucked Jared until he bled and couldn't even feel it. They'd found it funny as hell, but the next day he was in a world of pain. And the scabs . . .

Like a professional dope fiend, Todd snorted all four lines in succession, alternating nostrils like he was going to get a gold star for extra effort. He rubbed his nose and sniffed as meth sludge dripped down his throat. His sinuses became inflamed as the high rushed in, and all was right in the world.

An examination of his baggie assured him that he had enough in case there wasn't any good shit at the Blowout. Having never been to one, he didn't know what to expect. Figured it would be like a rave or some kind of ultra-secret dance party. If that was the case, there should be an array of drugs that would have impressed Hunter S. Thompson.

SICK! SICK! SICK!

Now that he'd powdered his nose, it was time to get ready for the Blowout. Had to look cool and sexy but in an elegant sort of way. Something to attract the right kind of guy, the kind that knew what he wanted and would go after it. In other words, a guy like himself. Todd had thought about how great it would be to have a man like him. Good-looking, intelligent, self-assured. Most guys he met were half-depressed and self-loathing. It got to be too much to take, so that's why he started on his mission of promiscuity: fuck 'em and fling 'em.

After an hour of trying on clothes to put together the right outfit and drinking shots of tequila to quell his mind from spinning out of control, Todd was ready.

He grabbed his phone and pulled up directions to the address on the card he was to bring and show at the door, mildly surprised to find that the Blowout was in the San Diego State University area. There were a lot of frat houses all around the school, but he wasn't aware of a gay fraternity.

It was about fifty blocks down El Cajon Boulevard, so he took the bus. It was better that way, in case he was too blitzed to drive afterward. If everything went the way he hoped, he would be spending the night in someone's bed playing a game of hide the hotdog in the buns, and parties like this one almost always had a happy ending.

The bus dropped him off on a street that left a lot to be desired. There were hookers who must have had finely tuned gaydar because they didn't even look at Todd, a group of homeless men having a get-together, a couple of guys walking with some kind of contrived swagger to either look cool or keep their oversized pants on, and any number of others walking around like their bodies were in some kind of pain.

Not Todd. He felt great, and he was dying of anticipation. He'd only *heard* of Blowout parties. Never even met someone who had been to one. No one really knew what went on, but the rumors were nothing short of pure, unadulterated ecstasy. He was kind of hoping for a four-course orgy. Wouldn't that be fun?

He crossed the busy street and headed closer to campus, marveling at the large Greek letters that symbolized fraternity names. He didn't go to college after high school like Chloe had. He figured he would go to design school or something, you know . . . after he partied for a few years. It had been more than a few, and though he made enough money with the online cam gig plus selling pills on the side, he really should strive for more.

He wouldn't have joined a fraternity anyway. It wasn't a place for the likes of him. That's why he was beginning to feel apprehensive about this little rendezvous. Just didn't seem like the kind of place for a Blowout party. The men in these dorms were fueled by cheap beer and testosterone, many of them trying to recreate the jocular magnitude of their high school days en masse. The girls, well, they were attention whores, the ones who wanted to be wanted and demanded to be liked. Not like Chloe at all. Todd had to admit that he had a bit of conceit in him, but he could do without Valley girls, thank you very much.

The house was nestled between two fraternities, one of them maybe 1,500 square feet, and the other maybe 2,000—small, older homes that had been converted to house the brothers and sisters of SDSU. Todd stood on the sidewalk before a large paved driveway sprinkled with cars, the red bookmark-sized card gripped in hand. He examined the address several times to be sure he wouldn't embarrass himself by knocking on the door of some unforgiving house of masculinity. The addresses matched.

What caused Todd pause were the towering Greek letters affixed to the balcony on the second floor. This was, indeed, a frat house.

"You're here for the Blowout too?" came a voice from behind, nearly causing Todd to jump.

He was tall and slender but looked like he worked out regularly. He had a quirky smile on his face—like he knew what to expect inside but couldn't believe he'd been invited—which was pretty much the way Todd felt about the whole ordeal.

"Yes, I am. This is the place then, huh?"

"I guess so."

The guy stuck out his hand and said, "I'm Frel."

"Frel? Really? That's your name?"

Frel's grin widened. "That so hard to believe?"

Todd shook his hand. "I'm Todd."

"Well, Todd, shall we go in?"

"Here goes nothing."

They could hear music as they stepped onto the front porch. After ringing the doorbell, a man opened the door and asked to see their invites. In exchange, he gave them each a small card instructing that they would need it later for pairing off.

"Ooooh, I wonder what that means," Todd said. On his card was printed *10 X*.

Pocketing the card, he took a look around. There were maybe fifteen people that he could see, mingling and sipping drinks out of Solo cups. Probably cheap beer. He certainly hoped they had a stocked bar so he could drink something a little more sophisticated than draft beer. And he didn't want some fruity tropical cocktail or blended ice drink. He wanted the real shit . . . maybe a bourbon on the rocks . . . that'd be nice.

As Todd made his way to the kitchen—where, from across the room, he saw a man dressed similarly to the guy who answered the door standing before a folding table with an array of liquor and a stack of red Solo cups—he took closer notice of the crowd. The music was loud, some kind of upbeat trance that got into your bones like electricity, demanding that you dance. There were some good-looking guys in the crowd. Some of them smiled and winked as Todd weaved through them on his way to the makeshift bar.

He asked for a whiskey on the rocks. Mechanically, the man poured his drink and handed him the red cup. Todd wasn't sure whether he was supposed to tip, but he didn't like the guy's attitude, or lack thereof, so he sipped his drink and turned to face the crowd.

After a few hours of drinking, hitting random joints that were floating through the crowd, and taking a couple of pills that may have been ecstasy, maybe valium, the Blowout began with an announcement.

"Excuse me, everyone!" a guy said through the PA system to the crowd of twenty or so facing him. At first, it struck Todd as strange that he looked like the doorman and the bartender, but he soon realized they were all from the fraternity, wearing shirts with their Greek symbols emblazoned on the front. They even wore their hair the same way, and there was something about their eyes . . . but that was crazy. The similarities had to stop with the clothes and haircuts, right?

The guy with the mic continued, "Have your Blowout cards ready, boys. This is the part of the night that's been known to get . . . messy." He giggled, as did most of the crowd, along with sounds of amusement and lewd comments. "Follow me into the Blowout room, boys. When we get in there, pair up with whoever has the same number as you. One of you will have an *X* by your number and one with an *O*."

They all filed through the kitchen, where there was a large door that had been opened. Through the door was a small hall leading to a building that had been built onto the back of the house. The walls were painted black and adorned with colorful signs displaying frat slogans. A large banner in the shape of a penis that stretched proudly on the center of one wall said "BLOWOUT" in bold letters across the shaft, with glittery semen that sparkled under the overhead lights jetting out of the tip.

Maybe it was the drugs, but everything seemed to be moving at varying rates of speed. Todd laughed at the phallic sign on the wall and then someone bumped into him, saying something like, "Hey lover, what card do you have?"

He dug the card out of his pocket. "Ten *X*," he said.

The guy pouted his lip. "I'm a two *X*."

Frel came by, card in hand. He gave Todd a seductive pair of eyes. "You a nine?"

"Ten."

"Oh well. Could have had fun together."

Soon enough, Todd was paired with one of the frat boys who had the *10 O* card. As the others were paired off, he asked a few questions.

"So you belong to this fraternity, right? What's your name?"

"I'm Brady. Yeah, I'm a brother."

"Hi, I'm Todd. You've got quite a body on you, Brady. I think they gave me the right card. How many Blowouts have you been to?"

Brady smiled, staring eagerly into Todd's eyes. "Every one of them. All in this room."

"They get pretty wild, right? That's what I've heard."

"Oh yeah. Sure to be a *blast*."

Todd wasn't sure what they were doing. Should he try to kiss this guy or wait for instruction? He'd been involved with so many men, and there were plenty of meth and fuck parties he'd gone to where maybe five guys would shoot and snort meth and just screw all night.

"You do speed?" asked Todd.

Brady shook his head. "Doesn't agree with me."

Todd smirked. It was always a letdown when he met a guy who wasn't into meth. That was some serious shit, mingling with his own kind. Dopers did better with dopers, plain and simple. But Todd always made an exception when it came to a gorgeous man, and this guy was all muscles and abs, a real health-conscious and athletic beefcake. Explains why he didn't mess with drugs.

"Mind if I have a quick hit?"

"Be my guest."

Todd pinched some dope from his bag and placed it on the back of his hand in sloppy mounds. He snorted it in two quick inhales and was pleased with the rush. This was that great blue ice shit that would keep him up for at least three days before he crashed out for maybe twenty-four hours straight.

"All right, boys," came the voice of the MC. "We're all paired up, so that means the Blowout is officially beginning, and it always begins with a ceremonial blowjob. So all of you with an

X on your card, get on your knees!" He giggled, as did many of the participants.

Brady gave Todd a look that pretty much said, "On your knees, fucker!" And so he obliged.

Todd figured he was a champion dick sucker. Had been doing it for as long as he'd been comfortable with his sexual orientation. Figured if he could get a few ribs removed like he'd heard Marilyn Manson did back in the nineties, he'd suck his own dick just to see how good he was.

"Get ready to have your mind blown," Todd said as he dropped to his knees.

"That's what a Blowout is all about," Brady said, staring down at Todd and smiling.

Todd didn't waste time. He unbuckled Brady's belt with vigor, practically using his teeth to unbutton his pants and pull down his boxers. He could feel the tightness of Brady's erection, his mouth just about salivating. He liked giving almost as much as receiving, and it was always the best right after snorting dope. He pulled out Brady's cock and marveled at the size of it. He mumbled something like, "Impressive," before deep-throating and almost gagging on it.

The room was filled with a dozen pairs of men, all performing the act of fellatio. The music in the air was moans of pleasure mixed with some amused giggles and the occasional gag.

After a few minutes, Todd thought Brady's penis was getting bigger in his mouth. He could swear the head was becoming engorged, and for a moment, he just about lost his shit. Almost panicked because he felt like he couldn't breathe, but he could. He could breathe out of his nose. He didn't want to be embarrassed by having a panic attack while giving head because he was a goddamn pro cocksucker.

But he knew it for sure now. Brady's member was definitely growing in his mouth—inflating like a balloon.

Fuck it, he thought, *I'll just work it harder, give it all I got, and he'll love me for it. He'll return the favor.*

But it got so big it hurt. Todd kept going, slobber dripping down his chin like a hungry Saint Bernard, partially choking when he drew the massive erection in too deep. He shifted his eyes to see as much of the room as he could, and something wasn't right. It took a minute to figure it out, but what he realized was that the frat boys were all standing. That's when he realized he had been lured there, like the others, to give these guys blowjobs, which wasn't a bad scam when you got right down to it. Frat boys could pull that shit off.

But the pain was intensifying. His jaw hurt and he was reminded of lying in a dentist's chair with his mouth held open by metal clamps. He'd gotten lockjaw when he had his wisdom teeth removed. Fearing that would happen again, he decided to pull Brady's dick out of his gullet for a breather.

But he couldn't!

The head of Brady's shaft had become so engorged that it was like shoving a fist in Todd's mouth. He was unable to get it out and he began to panic. The pain in his jaw intensified and he could taste coppery blood. Could have been his teeth biting into Brady's dick, could have been his teeth loosening. Whatever it was, it was bad news.

Brady stroked his hair. "*Shhhhh*. I know it hurts, but it'll be over soon. Enjoy it as much as you can."

Todd's eyes darted around the room. Everyone on their knees appeared to be in pain, squirming and flailing. Knelt down at Todd's left was Frel, his face bloated around a tree stump protruding from a frat boy's pubic hair. Todd looked at the guy and when he saw his eyes, he knew they were all in a heaping pile of doom. The eyes weren't human. They were glossed over and cloudy gray, and when he looked up at Brady, he saw the same inhuman eyes staring down at him. The grin on his face was so wide. Too wide! As if his skull had been restructured into something alien.

Todd whimpered as Brady made obnoxious noises through gritted teeth. Could have been pain, could have been pleasure.

Just as Todd felt as if his head would explode, there was a *pop* like an amplified champagne cork ringing in the New Year. The sound was so sudden and loud that Todd flinched, which caused his jaw to crack. He screamed as much as he could with his mouth around a massive love muscle. Realizing while doing so that everyone kneeling was screaming horrid, muffled screams laced with agony and sheer terror.

"Keep going, boy," Brady said. "You're doing so good. It'll be over soon. Just keep at it."

Brady gyrated, face fucking Todd faster, fistfuls of hair held tight to ensure his thrusts reached maximum depth. At this point, Todd wasn't doing anything; couldn't do anything but writhe and flail and hope something would alleviate his pain.

Todd kept eyeing Frel, but nothing was changing. They locked eyes just as another *pop* erupted from the room, this time followed by a loud, satisfied groan that was unmistakably indicative of great pleasure. They kept staring at one another, seemingly hanging onto some shredded bit of hope that connected them in this madhouse.

And then it happened. Frel's eyes grew into tiny balloons just before his head exploded. It was like a watermelon with a firecracker embedded within, except the splatter wasn't sweet fruit but brain matter, skull bits, and salty blood. The *pop* as his head exploded was the same as those Todd had heard earlier, only louder in this proximity. And then came more. As heads exploded all around him, Todd tried not to think about the warm flecks of blood and brain spattering him.

"Almost there," Brady said. "Get ready for your blowout."

The pressure increased tenfold like an instantaneous headache swelling in Todd's skull. His eyes grew wide as he choked, unable to breathe. Heat enveloped his face like a high-grade fever. Towering above him, Brady's grin stretched too wide. His reptilian eyes stared down like obsidian. Just as

Todd was on the verge of losing consciousness from lack of oxygen to his brain, it happened. Brady's engorged member swelled once again as his load was released, traveling from the base of his massive cock and shot out the tip with a muffled *pop* that exploded through Todd's head, ripping his cranium open in a blast of gore.

The frat boys took seats, exhausted from the yearly ritual, the smell of blood and semen heavy in the air. They watched as the demon seeds wiggled their way through the human pulp, finding corpses to nestle within for their gestation.

Pacify Her

The saccharine tone of his voice was childish when he told her his name was Tommy, but it took a few minutes for Alexis to realize that he was, indeed, a man regressed to the mind of an infant.

He asked what he could do for a grand. She told him for a grand he could do whatever he wanted, but she wasn't prepared for this kind of twisted fetish. Alexis had been walking the streets for five years now, and it showed. At thirty-one, she looked like a horse's ass, all hard lines and sunken cheeks; the evidence of drug abuse and copious amounts of liquor as futile attempts to stifle what had become of her and to enable her to sell her ass on the streets for enough money to support the monkey on her back and pay the rent, in that order.

In those five years, she'd seen all kinds of sick fucks: foot freaks, anal enthusiasts, masochists, and more. Tommy was something else altogether.

After putting on an oversized diaper and a bib, Tommy pulled a large rattle from his bag of tricks. He made small talk, literally, by blathering goo goos and gibberish, allowing drool to run from his mouth in a thick, sickening strand over his chubby face.

Alexis was uncomfortable in her bindings. It wasn't often that she allowed men to bind her, but a thousand bucks for an hour of kink was well worth it compared to a night of twenty-dollar blowjobs. But there was something in this man's eyes that frightened her.

As he rummaged through his bag of goodies, Alexis's stomach sank. What was going to be next? The blond-haired brute's arsenal of "toys" were oversized versions of things her six-month-old son held dear. She couldn't help but wonder if Tommy was pissing and shitting his diaper like an infant. Would he want her to change his diaper? She'd need more than a thousand if he wanted her to touch him after he'd been shitting himself.

Tommy produced an oversized pacifier. Alexis groaned. The last thing she did before leaving her son with Joan Rawls in the apartment next to hers was put his favorite pacifier in his mouth. He was so happy to have it that it broke her heart how she had to hustle to make ends meet. Sure, she waitressed part-time—no one was giving full-time work anymore—but that hardly paid the rent, much less bought groceries. Living was hard, and quitting the booze and dope for the sake of her son forced her to become aware of what she was doing to herself. A year ago, she would have been high and submissive. When a John had finished he would leave, and while waiting for the cum to dry on her face, she would suck on a crack pipe to forget.

Now, nothing was forgotten.

Tommy didn't put the pacifier in his mouth as she suspected he would. His cheery face of baby blissfulness dropped to something akin to madness, which filled Alexis with horror. Tommy closed in on her, gripping the large pacifier in a beefy workingman's hand, the bulbous end pointed toward Alexis.

She had been in sketchy situations before, sometimes succumbing to things she wasn't proud of to get away from potential danger. Things beyond that of *normal* prostitution. She'd been beaten, abused, her body violated and torn, but there was something about this man, something about his proclivities that frightened the hell out of her. Or perhaps it was the harsh realities of turning weirdo tricks with a clean mind.

"Please don't," Alexis said. All her years in the biz and she couldn't remember ever saying that. She had always been afraid the John would become angered, and anger quickly turned to hitting. But now that she had a son to care for, she was becoming more defensive.

Tommy's maniacal expression dropped. In a blubbery voice, he reminded her, "You said I could do whatever I wanted."

Alexis began weeping. She tried to stop herself, tried desperately to hide her fear. The Johns preyed on fear. She opened her mouth to protest further, but she didn't get a chance before the pacifier was thrust into her maw. It didn't fit, but Tommy was determined, so he crammed it in as Alexis flailed her head from side to side trying to scream. Tommy became furious, gritting his teeth. He pushed and jammed until the junction of her lips and cheeks split to allow the pacifier entrance.

Eyes wide and glossing over with tears, Alexis screamed, which only resulted in her cheeks ripping further. Shock dulled the pain, for now at least. Had there been a mirror for her to see the state of her face, she would have lost her shit. Due to her bindings, she couldn't move, and even if she could have made noise, it wasn't likely that someone would bother checking on her here. This motel was a shithole notorious for drugs and prostitution. The police didn't even mess with this place.

Tommy smiled like a loon, blowing bubbles from his slobbery mouth. Alexis struggled with her bindings, but there was no way she was going to free herself. Tears cascaded down her face, mixing with the blood from her torn cheeks before dripping onto her bare shoulders and breasts. She tried pleading with him, but her words were lost in the pacifier gag. Not that he would oblige.

"Now," Tommy said in an obnoxious childlike voice, "time for da baby to eat."

He reached into his bag once again. Alexis screamed into the pacifier, snot bubbling from her nose. Her cheeks burned as salty tears entered the cracks where her flesh split.

"Ooooh," Tommy said as he pulled out something Alexis didn't immediately recognize. Not until he came closer did she realize that he was holding a large, queerly shaped bulb syringe, like the one she'd used to clear her son's runny nose when he had a cold a week ago, though this one had an awkward dual tip. It was a bizarre contraption of Tommy's creation that looked more like a torture device than an obscene infant snot-sucking tool.

Tommy looked Alexis square in the eyes. "You wanna help baby eat?"

She shook her head, weeping. The shock was beginning to wear off, causing her face to feel like a red-hot branding iron that pulsed with her heartbeat.

"Anything baby wants, right? Baby paid. Baby gets what baby wants."

Tommy's left hand lunged at Alexis, grabbing a fistful of her hair, knuckles against her skull. With his right hand, he held the modified bulb syringe. The dual tip of brass stared at Alexis as he held her head in position, the device closing in on her face. She attempted to squirm and flail, but her position was so compromised that she could do nothing to thwart Tommy's twisted desires.

The bulb syringe had a handle on it with a trigger, which, when pulled, caused the large bulb to implode, blowing the excess air out, cool against Alexis's angry, swollen cheeks. The cold brass tips touched Alexis's nose almost playfully at first.

Tommy tried to be gentle, but her head was difficult to hold still. His goofy smile deteriorated once again, replaced with anger. His grip on the handle tightened as he thrust the dual brass tips of the bulb syringe into her nostrils until he was sure he had gained entrance to her brain. He then pulled the trigger, which began pressurizing the contraption, sucking the contents of her skull through the brass tips, slowly and noisily into the large bulb.

Alexis knew it was over. In that moment, she knew her son would be safe in the gentle hands of her neighbor, Joan Rawls. Probably better off than living a life subjected to Alexis's personal demons. She wanted only one thing in those seconds when the brass entered her nasal cavity and broke through her skull. Selfish as it was, she wanted a hit of crack to alleviate the pain, but then the lights went out, and her pain was muted forever.

Allen Hamm found the motel without trouble. It was in the part of town that reeked of urine and vomit that was more cheap wine than regurgitated food. He wasn't even sure why he was there, why he gave a good goddamn about Alexis. He should have used the courts to go after the child and kicked her to the curb, but there was some part of him that still loved her despite her sordid life.

The lobby stunk. The man behind the desk had eyes as hollow and dark as empty gloves. He'd seen some shit, that's for sure. Lived it too.

Allen slapped a fifty on the grime-blackened counter. "Alexis. She has a room here. Which one is it?"

The man's eyes shifted in a downward gaze to the money, then back to Allen. "Number twenty-two. Second floor." The man grabbed the bill and pocketed it without breaking eye contact. "You never seen me."

Allen nodded and backed away, grateful to be out of reach of the man's funky breath. He took the hallway to a stairwell that was decorated with bottles in brown paper bags and needles, with a rail-thin man shivering in withdrawal. Real high class.

What the hell am I doing here?

He had been so pissed off when he found out about Alexis's *real* profession. How she'd hid it from him for so long, he didn't know. He worked the graveyard shift at the plant, so it sort of made it easy for her to turn tricks while he turned screws. The meth kept her awake and then she would crash for twenty-four to forty-eight hours at a time. He could deal with the drugs; he'd had a drinking problem of his own and even did coke from time to time for fun. He thought she would quit the meth in the name of love, and she was very convincing when she wanted to be, but when he learned of the prostitution, he was sick to his stomach. At first, he didn't believe it when Joan told him.

In fact, he figured she was just bitter due to some neighborly conflict, and he was furious at her for spreading lies.

They weren't lies.

And now Allen found himself walking down the hallway of the second floor to room twenty-two, the room Alexis used when a John wanted something more than a quick blowjob in the backseat of a car. The same neighbor who had informed Allen of Alexis's streetwalking also informed him that she'd birthed his baby. Again, he was distraught and suspended in a state of disbelief, but the neighbor kept calling him. Told him she was a nurse and could perform a paternity test if he was willing to have his mouth swabbed. All this a year after he had left the whore and moved on. He wasn't even sure he wanted to know if the child was his, but he knew he would take that regret to the grave were he not to find out.

Room twenty-two. The door was stained with fluids and fingerprints, much like everything else in this filth bucket. She was in there. Probably bare-assed and spread-eagled with some overweight and undereducated bastard grunting as he thrust into her. Allen was no Dirty Harry, but he brought a gun in case there was any trouble. Not that he anticipated problems. The John would probably be so mortified he would collect his clothes and flee. What Allen was uncertain about was the response from Alexis. He figured he would let her know everything and tell her he would give their relationship one last chance if she would quit selling her body. When her neighbor told him she had cleaned up her drug and alcohol habit since the birth of their child, Allen thought maybe what they shared a year ago could be rekindled. He had loved her before he found out about the prostitution. He was no angel, what with his checkered past of drinking and coke and slinging dick on the sleazier dating apps, but he was ready for a change. If she left the biz, he could imagine living life together as a family and raising their son. Deep inside, he knew Alexis was a good woman, and he could be her Prince Charming, crazy as it sounded. He believed in second chances, and he had his AA two-years-sober token to prove it.

When he kicked the door open, he saw something that sank his gut and took his breath away. Everything flashed before his eyes: visions of happiness, of raising their child together, of a life with the only woman he had ever fallen in love with.

A man dressed like a baby was sitting on the floor with his legs crossed, sucking on a sippy cup and making obnoxious slurping noises. His maw was pink from a mixture of slobber and blood dripping from his chin, grotesquely saturating his oversized diaper stained yellow in the front with liquid shit oozing out the sides and smeared on his hairy legs like a melted Hershey's bar.

Next to the sicko was Alexis's naked body strapped to a chair. Her head was tilted down, but Allen could see that she was gagged. There was an awful lot of blood on her face and chest, along with something that looked like mucus and blood clots or brain matter. On a table near her body was a blender coated with a disgusting, bloody mess. Beside it lay a strange contraption with a small pool of blood beneath it saturating a pile of C-notes.

In his blissful sucking of the blended brain food, Tommy hadn't noticed Allen's entrance. He merely sat there on the floor enjoying the fruits of his one-thousand-dollar exploit when Allen disturbed him by asking, "What the fuck happened here? What did you do to her?"

Tommy's head shot up, lips slathered with brain goop, his sippy cup now on the carpet. "What are you doing here?" he asked, lips trembling, eyes wide, his voice sad and childlike.

Allen drew his gun. He had never drawn a gun on anyone in his life. Never thought he'd have to.

"Don't shoot! I paid. I paid. She said I could do anything for a thousand dollars. Anything!"

The gun trembled in Allen's hands. His nerves shattered. He could off the sick bastard and be done with it. Probably no one would suspect much, considering the neighborhood and the reputation of the motel, but he had a son to think about. A son who was now without a mother.

He lowered his weapon and walked further into the room, gaining momentum as he zeroed in on Tommy.

"I paid, I pa—"

Thwack! Allen pistol-whipped Tommy hard enough to drag a ragged gash across his head and laid him out cold.

He called the police. As much as he wanted to shoot the man, he had his son to consider. The boy needed his father. He needed a good life, and that was something Allen wouldn't be able to give him behind prison bars.

He pulled out his AA token that proved he had two years' sobriety under his belt and tossed it onto Alexis's bloody lap as a tear ran down his face.

Wrapped in Plastic

Clinton and Rand were two of the dumber sons of bitches you were likely to meet in rural East Tennessee, what with ten teeth between them and inbred faces that gave the appearance of the kind of goons who would have a bright future sucking the government's titty and impregnating their cousins at family barbeques after too many Busch Lights.

They were brothers, Clinton and Rand. Lived on the family land, all of five acres that housed several generations of Dunns. Clinton lived in an RV that smelled like a horse barn, and Rand lived in the fucking horse barn that smelled like cat piss and mold. Clinton had managed to keep a job for a few months a while back, scrounging enough money to buy the RV. He'd planned on getting the sumbitch running again but lost his job when his boss caught him jerking to the Tractor Supply ad in the storeroom. He had the ad open to a country girl with a cowboy hat and boots, but she couldn't have been a day over ten.

SICK! SICK! SICK!

Clinton and Rand were that rare breed of redneck who didn't know how to work on cars, though Uncle Skids did. Problem was, Uncle Skids was doing time for home invasion. Then there was their father, Gary, who was a carpenter. He was one of the only Dunns who made an honest living. He was a handy grease monkey but could hardly find the time for his boys, they being such disappointments and all.

Most the time, Clinton and Rand liked to hunt. There was that one year they mistook cousin Laura for a sickly doe and put an arrow right through her. The boys had been high on meth. They saw movement and Rand pulled his bow. Turned out Laura was just poppin' a squat out in the woods. By the time they got to her, she was dead, her ass awash in liquid shit.

There really wasn't a sensible person in the Dunn family. Even Gary, the only one to make a proper living, was as slow as a slug on summer pavement. That day, when Rand put an arrow through cousin Laura, the boys had to make one of the most important decisions of their lives. A decision that turned into an argument. Clinton suggested burning her body, while Rand thought burying her would be more dignified. Clinton was smart enough to know that burying her would leave remains, and what if someone came looking? But burning her would create a problem all its own. Would the fire be hot enough to turn bone to dust?

That day, they'd stood there looking down at Laura's body akimbo on the ground, shit-spattered ass, arrow through her back and protruding from her breast, the blood having soaked her shirt and plastered it to her wiry frame. Her face had been kind of cocked up, mouth in a rictus of terror that showed off a set of plaque-covered chompers like a braying donkey's. It wasn't her best look, but then again, it wasn't her worst.

Eventually, they decided to bring her to the trash pile. The one they pushed directly into the river. They rationalized that if her body was found, it would be assumed she went for a swim and drowned. Problem was, they wrapped her body in plastic wrap to make it easier to carry, not once considering how that would look were her body to be discovered. Kin asked about Laura, but she was never seen again. Clinton and Rand acted stupid when questioned, which is to say they didn't act at all. Laura was assumed to have gone off on a tweak binge, never to return.

The river in question was really more like a glorified creek. Water ran good in some parts and slowed to a crawl in others. The amount of garbage that was dumped in the river, as well as countless leaching septic tanks, caused a layer of film to settle on the river rocks. The edges were foamy and often strewn with debris that hadn't caught the right current and gone downstream.

Next to shooting guns, hunting, and sticking their peckers in places they didn't belong, those boys loved swimming.

"Hey, Clint?" Rand said, squinting his beady eyes in a face that was beer-bloated and red. "You ever think about where this river runs?"

Clinton stood there, waist-deep in murky water, and pondered that as if it was the very question of life itself. His jaw moved, but that wasn't a sign of thoughtfulness, just a twitch the meth fairy left him.

"I guess it probably meets up with a bigger river somewhere."

"Yeah, but where?"

"Down yonder, you dumbfuck. Where else? All this shit goes to the Tennessee River anyhow. I think."

"Why don't we go down and see where it ends?"

"What the hell for?"

"Just curious."

"You know what curiosity did to the cat, you stupid fuck?"

Rand stared at Clinton, mouth agape, eyes sort of squinted. The living embodiment of a big, dumb question mark.

Clinton sighed. "The fuck did curiosity do to the cat? Fuck if I know. Probably killed the little bastard." Clinton swallowed the last of the beer he'd been drinking and dropped the can in the water. "Okay, fuck it. Let's float downstream and see where we end up. We can walk back on land."

And so the Dunn boys went on a little adventure.

As they floated with the current, Rand liked to drag his feet across the slimy bedrock. The slickness made him think of when they had those three hogs: Sally, Jesse, and Raphael. After a good rain, the boys would jump in the pigs' pen and chase them around, trying to grab hold of their slippery little piggy bodies, laughing as the swine scrambled for safety. The pigs would get real worked up. One time, Clinton had Rand grab Sally and hold her still by the head while Clinton came from behind. You'd have thought he was about to go to town on the prom queen by the size of his rod. Sally didn't like it at all. She squealed and shifted and Clinton was having the time of his life once he got his rhythm down. That was, until Sally bit Rand on his fat, inbred face. Rand let go of her and she pulled away from Clinton just as he let go of his load, and goddamn, that was a sight. Something Rand would never forget. He was laughing so hard he forgot how bad his face hurt.

So yeah, Rand liked the sliminess of the bedrock, and he had his reasons.

Clinton took the lead. That's how it always was, he being the older brother and all. They'd only ventured so far in the past, mostly by land, mostly while hunting. He wasn't skittish about anything. However, he didn't appreciate the slimy bedrock like his brother did. If anything, he would have liked to come across a dead trout. Clinton was a horny motherfucker. He used to sneak off and use dead trout like a pocket pussy. He got the idea from that movie *American Pie*, but when he stuck his dick in an apple pie, it turned into a gooey mess and he caught hell from Momma. One day, he found a dead trout on the riverbank. The body was soft enough to push his finger through, yet firm enough not to crumble apart in his hands. He thought of that damn movie and had a lightbulb moment, as well as an erection.

Rand caught wind of what his brother had been doing and started calling him "Fishfucker." That was, until Clinton had enough and beat his brother's ass real good. Rand was crying like a baby, all bloody and missing a few more teeth. Clinton threatened to fuck him in the ass, but he ended up smearing a rotten fish all over Rand's body instead. A *used* rotten fish, if you know what I'm getting at.

As they traveled farther, the riverbanks became more covered in yellow foam and littered with random pieces of refuse. Rand found a Mountain Dew can caught by a tree branch that was tangled within the clutches of a rock pile. He grabbed it and beamed.

"Hey, Clint, look at this! This was our can from last week."

Clinton turned to look at his brother. "Don't be so ignorant. There's all kinds of cans out here."

"But look! It has the burn marks from where we smoked weed out of it. It's *our* can!"

Clinton trudged through the water back to where his brother stood, proudly waving the green soda can.

"Sumbitch," Clinton said. "That sure is our can. Wish we had some weed to smoke out of it now."

Rand tossed the can into the river and watched it float downstream like a little green boat, besting the tiny rapids and then swooping around a large bend. The water was deeper now but still only waist-high. They'd floated most of the way, trying to save their feet from the abuse of slipping and sliding across the bedrock. They'd been in the river enough to know that slick bedrock resulted in twisted toes and scraped ankles.

"Wanna go any further?" Rand asked.

"Just around the bend," Clinton said. "I'm getting bored."

"Me too."

"Momma's making squirrel and dumplings."

Rand pouted, "She making enough for us?"

"Well, hell, she better. I killed her five squirrels yesterday." Clinton continued floating downstream. "Come on, shit for brains."

Rand followed.

Around the bend, they ran into something fascinating, something that made the journey worth every second.

"What the fuck is that?" Clinton asked.

The water rounded the bend swiftly, then calmed to a placid state. Up ahead was something they both thought was a beaver dam, but turned out to be man-made. The boys floated closer, the water getting deeper. They could barely touch the bottom.

"Holy fuck, Clint, I didn't know the river got this deep."

"Don't be a pussy."

"I'm not, it's just—"

"Shut the fuck up, Rand. What the hell is this?"

Before them was a blockage that water could only seep through or breach from around the edges. As the boys approached, both of them became wary, for they could now see that this was no beaver dam. Instead of being created of branches and twigs and leaves, this blockage was made from years of garbage that had floated downstream, all packed together into a tight mass that dammed off the water to create a deep pool.

"This is kind of cool," Clinton said, but there was no conviction in his voice.

"I don't know, Clint."

Then Clinton scrunched up his face. "Kind of smells, don't it?"

Rand nodded.

They tried to stay away from the dam of human refuse, but it seemed as if the bedrock fell from beneath their feet. They were floating like turds in a toilet bowl, and the water around them smelled about as bad, like raw sewage. Daddy had run the gray water to drain into the river, but they'd always thought the toilets were on septic.

Rand started panicking. "It's pulling me!"

"Oh, stop whining. You're such a—"

Then Clinton was swept into the pull. He tried to play it cool, but soon enough, he was flailing around and struggling to swim. The water was so placid, so still, and yet something was pulling them toward the dam. As they got closer, they could feel things beneath the murky water. Slimy things that slithered across their legs. There was no bottom, but their feet seemed to drag through debris that had sunk, yet floated around in the mire. The water bubbled and garbage floated to the top, only to become submerged again: milk cartons, beer cans, plastics, waterlogged pieces of cardboard, fast-food wrappers, and pieces of broken glass.

The boys kicked their legs and flailed their arms, trying desperately to swim out of there, but they made no traction. The water pulled them toward the wall of garbage no matter what they did.

"What the fuck, Rand?"

Rand cried, "I can't get out!"

"Swim! We can get out of this!"

"I can't!"

They floated through the roiling water until they both smacked into the dam, slapping against the slimy face and sticking to the gummy surface like a couple flies on a gooey fly trap.

"What the fuck is this?" Rand asked.

Clinton shook his head.

There were garbage bags intertwined with the discards of their daily lives. All the Mountain Dew and Busch Light cans. The milk and egg cartons. The fast-food wrappers. All there, all entangled in a tightly packed wall that blocked the flow of the river and created a cesspool.

"Maybe we can climb up this shit," Clinton said. "Or even just hang on and guide ourselves to the side."

"I can't move, Clint. I can't move!"

Clint grimaced, putting all his strength into moving, but it was as if some kind of pull held them firmly in place. That was when something emerged from the wall of the dam. A thread that grew thicker as it materialized, now more like a rope, protruding from the dam inch by inch, each foot of the substance tied together like sheets a teenager throws out of their second story window to sneak out at night, only this bizarre thread was made entirely out of food wrappers, all tied together into a neat rope that was a good five feet between the boys, swirling around about a foot above the water.

Rand started to say something, but his voice came out about as screechy as a whining sow. The rope of wrappers whipped around and smacked Rand in the face, almost as if telling him to shut the fuck up. It then curled around his neck, wrapping itself around and around. Rand's eyes went wide.

"Oh fuck!" Clinton yelled. He reached to grab at the wrapper rope, but something slithered out of the slimy dam of refuse and grabbed his hand. It was green and black and unpleasant, but clearly a *hand* that grabbed him. His mouth dropped and he started crying. He'd been a tough guy right up to that point, but his nerves were shaken to the core of his black heart.

The hand was mottled and rotted, but the arm was still wrapped in plastic.

Rand struggled to breathe. The rope of food wrappers squeezed tighter. His face turned blue. The wrapper rope loosened its grip, allowing Rand to gulp some air. On the other side, something was birthed from the wall of trash, something big and nasty. It was human-like in form but created of bones. The head was a deer skull, white showing through blackened skin that had rotted and hung off in strips. The body was a mix of bones from birds and deer and cattle, all fused together with tendon-like threads of offal. An arm reached around, the hand a mess of half-eaten chicken legs and fish spines.

Rand squirmed and choked on his words as the rope of food wrappers lifted him out of the water and pulled him so that his back was against the top of the dam, his fat belly bobbing in the water, legs kicking beneath.

Beside Rand, Clinton was immobile, the hand of their cousin holding him firmly in place. While the creature of old bones emerged, so did Laura. Her face was still wrapped in plastic, fat maggots trapped beneath and wriggling as if her gaping mouth was a giant speaker emitting dance music for the larvae. The hollows where her eyes had been seemed to stare right at Clinton. The look on what was left of her face, now a puffy mush of doughlike flesh, was the same braying donkey visage he last saw when he looked down at her lifeless body covered in shit and blood.

Lying atop the dam, Rand looked up at the treetops that crowned the river and the blue sky beyond with wisps of white clouds. He tried to find peace but could feel the dam beneath his back shifting and pulsing as something within took shape. Something worse than the bone-creature, or cousin Laura wrapped in Visqueen. He saw it snake up from the top of the dam. A length of spines fused together with everything from electrician's tape to soiled bandages to pieces of chewing gum. They were the spines of fowl and fish looming over Rand. He screamed, and that's when it entered his body through his toothless maw, diving deep and twisting like a plumbing snake. Rand's screams came out muffled as his body shook from the force of the spines spinning through his guts, churning his insides, and then the fused-bone weapon tore through Rand's pelvis, pushing his wet shorts down as it emerged. The length of spines bursting through the aperture in a splatter of red chunks, spinning like a drill, annihilating intestines and organ meat.

After watching his brother eviscerated, Clinton scrambled more urgently to get away, but he was pinned in place. Laura's plastic-wrapped face was right beside him, her mouth close to his ear like she were about to whisper something to him. From the other side, her right arm presented itself, this one torn free from her plastic bonds, the fingers thick and waterlogged but strange, in that they were covered with shards of green, brown, and clear glass from the many beer bottles the Dunn boys had tossed in the river.

Laura's glittering right hand teased Clinton at first, tapping his forehead and cheeks just hard enough to make little cuts, for the glass was razor-sharp. She then used her forefinger and swiped one of his eyes. Clinton screamed. Blood and ocular fluid drained from the damaged eye, further blurring his vision. Another finger sliced through his cheek, opening it all the way to his gums. Her pinky had a thin sliver of glass like a sharpened fingernail. That one went into his nose, jammed up there like a vicious cotton swab.

Clinton screamed, and then the glass-speckled hand swiped across his throat, opening it up in ribbons of severed flesh, blood spilling into the nasty river water as Clinton gurgled on the last vestiges of his life. Laura maneuvered herself to a sitting position on the top of the dam above Clinton. As he choked on his own blood, she unwrapped a portion of her plastic shroud, placed it over his head, and wrapped it around his face.

Now, the Dunn boys were the trash everyone knew them to be.

About the Author

Robert Essig is the author of 21 books including Baby Fights, This Damned House, Broth House, and Secret Basements. He has published over 100 short stories and edited three small press anthologies. You can find him at various social media outlets such as Facebook, TikTok and BlueSky. Subscribe to Robert's newsletter for free for updates on his work. Robert lives with his family in east Tennessee.

Also by Robert Essig

This Damned House is a collection of four novelettes bound with a wraparound story of the strange man who lives in the house upon the hill, forever obsessing over the people of Greenwood Planes.

Clean Freak

Growing up in filth can make a clean freak out of anyone, but what can even the most avid housekeeper do against a verminous invasion that seems to come out of nowhere?

Behind the Greasepaint
Brazzy the Clown is a drunk. After another abysmal birthday party, she decides to finally commit to killing herself, only she finds that Death doesn't want her yet.

As I Lay Rotting
What happens when a couple of aging goths start to rot from the outside in? Can they get away from the threat at their door that wants their putrid flesh?

Photo-Graphic Content
It started with a picture of his son molesting the family dog. Then more pictures showed up. Then videos. Soon a tight-knit family of four turn on one another as horrific secrets are unveiled.

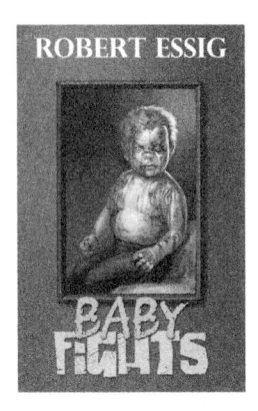

Would you pay to watch babies fight to the death?

Only the wealthy and privileged have the kind of money that can pay for such vile entertainment. The first rule of Baby Fights is there are no rules. Babies can't follow rules. But with a certain persuasion they turn into rabid little monsters, and oh what a spectacle it is to see.

Two babies enter the ring. Only one comes out alive. The only rule of Baby Fights is that one must die. Always.

Would you pay to watch babies kill each other in the ring? Oh, you don't have that kind of money? Then open this book and read about it.

SICK! SICK! SICK!

Everyone has a unique voice, a unique story. And sometimes those stories are twisted, bent, horrific . . . infected!

Smell the magic in the blood-smeared mirrors of a desolate bathroom wall.
Feel the pain of a thick hair that grows from your back and threatens your family!
Taste the rising gorge as a group of unknown assailants try to achieve a sick world record.
See the crusty landscape of a man covered in scabs!
Feel the rush of a simulated car wreck gone wrong.
Smell the pungent aroma of huffing death in a jar!
Taste the fruits of a cannibal feast.

Everyone has a voice. Some voices are sicker than others. Some stories should never be told.

The clowns aren't always happy.
The players sometimes get played.
Fitting in hurts.
When the cab locks and you can't get out.
When gambling brings you to a dark, dark place.
When inflatable animals are your best friends.

That's when you're infected.

These are the stories from Infected Voices.

Printed in Great Britain
by Amazon